Jake woke with a start only a short time later, when Kim came in with Dede in her arms.

He heard her putting Dede down in her crib, and waited to open his eyes when she came into his field of vision. He heard her approach and looked up.

The first thing he saw was an angel. The light was behind her and it made her golden hair glow as it flew wildly about her pretty face. Her fur coat added to the illusion. And then she threw it off and revealed her trim figure in its slightly snug nurse's uniform and wiped him out for good. He hadn't known he had this thing for nurses. Who knew?

"How are you doing?" she asked, bending over him. "I'll bet you're hungry."

He shook his head and risked a quick look at her. "Not really," he said. She was close enough to touch, so he was going to have to keep his response to her reined in. He groaned and half laughed at himself. He could barely move, much less make a play for a beautiful woman. Besides, he despised her. He kept forgetting that.

Dear Reader

So what's so great about royalty, anyway? They're just people who happen to be born into a situation a little luckier than the rest of us. They're not usually any better-looking than we are. They're definitely not any smarter. Or more talented. Or kinder, or better or harder-working. So why do we care about them?

But we do. They fascinate us. From earliest childhood we listen to fairytale stories of handsome heroic princes rescuing beautiful princesses from dark towers. We look at them and hope to see how a charmed set of people, elevated above everyday concerns, operates on a higher level than the one we inhabit.

The funny thing is, they so often disappoint us. They don't always slay the dragon, or rescue the captive hero, or protect the orphaned children from the witch. But they always seem to be running around in exotic locations, wearing stunning clothes and being treated like the celebrities they are. And all that just for being born into royalty.

So we watch with wide eyes and imagine what it would be like to live like that. They may not be any better than we are, but they certainly seem to be having more fun!

Long live fairytales!

Raye Morgan

THE RELUCTANT PRINCESS

BY
RAYE MORGAN

MILLS & BOON

First published in Great Britain 2012
by Mills & Boon, an imprint of Harlequin (UK) Limited.
Harlequin (UK) Limited, Eton House, 18-24 Paradise Road,
Richmond, Surrey TW9 1SR

© Helen Conrad 2012

ISBN: 978 0 263 22650 8

Raye Morgan has been a nursery school teacher, a travel agent, a clerk and a business editor, but her best job ever has been writing romances—and fostering romance in her own family at the same time. Current score: two boys married, two more to go. Raye has published over seventy romances, and claims to have many more waiting in the wings. She lives in Southern California, with her husband and whichever son happens to be staying at home at the moment.

Recent books by Raye Morgan:

CROWN PRINCE, PREGNANT BRIDE!
SINGLE FATHER, SURPRISE PRINCE!
SECRET PRINCE, INSTANT DADDY!
BEAUTY AND THE RECLUSIVE PRINCE
THE ITALIAN'S FORGOTTEN BABY
KEEPING HER BABY'S SECRET
HER VALENTINE BLIND DATE
FOUND: HIS ROYAL BABY
ABBY AND THE PLAYBOY PRINCE
THE PRINCE'S SECRET BRIDE
THE BOSS'S DOUBLE TROUBLE TWINS

This book is dedicated to Lauri
and her two little princesses, Kirsten and Kate.

CHAPTER ONE

KIM GUILDER stared out the bus window into the intense eyes of the stranger in the long leather coat. He was coming down the wide, stone stairway from the hospital administration building, moving like a man with a purpose, headed straight at her.

Her heart lurched and she looked quickly at the bus driver. Would he wait? Would the man make the bus?

But no. Relief filled her as the bus began to pull away from the curb. She reached out to steady herself on the handrail as it lurched into high speed. She looked back at the stalker, feeling a strange sense of triumph. He stood very still, staring after her. There was no way he could stop the bus, no way he could catch it and climb aboard. But she shivered in a quick attack of irrational fear anyway.

She didn't know him. She didn't think she'd ever seen him before. But he knew her. The way he'd been coming down those stairs when she'd looked up and caught sight of him, the way his eyes had blazed at her, she'd known right away he was trying to catch her. And she even thought she knew why.

She glanced around at the other passengers, wondering if anyone had noticed what had just happened. No one looked up except a little girl with bouncing red curls, sucking her thumb. The child stared at Kim, but dully, without significance.

Kim took a deep breath and tried to settle her pulse rate. What was she worried about, anyway? He'd caught sight of her there in that public area and obviously he'd recognized her right away. But that had to be pure coincidence. He couldn't possibly know where she was going or even the location of the rooms she was staying in right now. But something told her he would try.

Maybe she'd better find another place to stay, quickly. Maybe she should just race back to the rooms, grab her baby, and go.

But go where? It was coming down to that. There weren't many places left to run to.

She glanced back toward where they'd come from with a new spurt of adrenaline, suddenly wondering if he could find a way to follow the bus. No, how could he? It was almost impossible to find a taxi in this town, so unless he'd leaped up at the last minute and was clinging to the roof like an action hero, he had no hope.

So why wouldn't the butterflies in her stomach settle down? She looked out at the darkened streets. It was starting to snow. Half the streetlights were out, just another consequence of the recent war. But some optimistic souls had strung up Christmas lights here and there. It wasn't exactly cheerful, but it was a sign of survival.

She pulled her fake-fur coat more tightly around her and tried a couple of cleansing breaths, waiting, hoping, to feel a bit of calm return. She knew this was crazy. A man she didn't even know had picked up her world and tossed it into chaos for a moment or two. She couldn't let that sort of thing happen. She had a baby to think of.

But where had he come from so suddenly? His face,

his eyes, they looked so familiar. She didn't know who he was, but she knew two things about him: he knew exactly who she was, and he'd been sent by the Ambrian royal family, and that meant Pellea, who was now queen.

Pellea was one thing—this man was quite another. Those icy spikes of fear she'd felt were a direct response to the animosity in his eyes. He'd never met her before and he already hated her. What did that tell you about the relationship she had with the royal family?

It hadn't always been like that, at least, not with Pellea. They'd been best friends most of their lives, pampered children of the Granvilli regime which had toppled the royal family before they were born. And then Pellea fell in love with Crown Prince Monte DeAngelis and helped him invade the island, restoring the monarchy. And Kim was left behind to pick up the pieces and mend the fences—and take the brunt of the anger when the Granvillis began to lose.

Her stop was just ahead. She rose, hanging on to the metal bar and moving toward the back exit. She looked out into the dark street behind. Headlights swooped by, making her heart lurch every time, but no one seemed to linger. She stared harder into the night. She couldn't help it. She just had a feeling....

The bus slowed to a stop at the side of the slippery road. It seemed to take forever for the door to open, and when it did, she took a deep breath and headed out into the snowy night.

"Hello, Kimmee," a deep voice spoke from just be-hind her.

She whirled, shock rocketing through her soul. It couldn't be him. It was impossible. And yet...

There he stood, tall and dark and terrifying.

Her first instinct was to run. He saw it in her eyes and his hand clamped down on her upper arm.

"I need to talk to you."

She looked around quickly, trying to find someone who might help her, but the bus was leaving, its red taillights staring back impassively. Even more chilling, though cars rushed past anonymously, the street was empty of pedestrians. There was no one to run to. Her heart pounded.

"Let me go," she gasped at him. "I'm going to scream. The police…"

"The police are hard to find these days and you know it," he told her dryly, his eyes glittering in the light from the street lamp. "Besides, you don't need them. I'm not here to hurt you. I was sent to give you some important information. Something that could change your life."

She thought quickly. He was probably telling the truth. He wasn't the first who had been sent to try to convince her to come back to the castle. Each one seemed to have a more fantastic story meant to lure her away.

But this was a bit different. This one didn't like her.

She looked up at him, studying his face for a stealthy moment. How could he look so familiar at the same time she was so sure she'd never seen him before? Odd.

He was ridiculously handsome, with even features and a square jaw that bespoke a lack of tolerance for nonsense. His eyes were crystal blue and penetrating, framed by lush dark lashes any beauty queen would commit outlandish crimes to get for herself. Still, there was no hint of softness, not even a trace of any sort of compassion or sensitivity.

Everything about him telegraphed strength and authority, even a sense of command. And every one of those elements only made her feel more rebellious.

Still, he was bigger than she was, stronger than she was, and right now, he had hold of her arm. She figured it was useless to try to get away. Better to play along until she saw her chance.

"Okay, change my life," she said a bit sarcastically, looking at where his long fingers held her prisoner. "Tell me quickly. I've got to go."

His hold on her tightened.

"Where are you going?" he asked.

Looking up, she met his cold gaze and managed to keep from flinching. That was a plus.

There was no way she could let him know where she was staying. The rooms she'd taken were only a block away. Dede, her nine-month-old baby, was there with a babysitter she didn't completely trust. She had to get back to her right away. But letting this hostile man tag along was an impossibility. She felt trapped.

"Just tell me this important information you have for me," she said, trying to look as hard as he did while wiping snowflakes off her cheeks and shaking them from her thick blond hair. "And I'll be on my way."

The faint twist of his wide mouth almost looked like a smile, but there was no sign of that in his cold blue eyes.

"No chance," he said, then glanced up and down the dark street. Most of the shabby stores were closed, but a small café on the corner looked open.

"Let's go in there," he said, jerking his head in the direction of the coffee shop. "I'll buy you something warm to drink."

She tensed, firming her resistance. Maybe if she

showed him she was no pushover he would tell her quickly and leave her alone. Maybe.

"I don't want a drink or anything else," she told him crisply. "I don't know who you are or where you came from. If you've got information for me, why don't you send it to me in a letter?" Her chin rose and she glared at him as fiercely as she knew how.

He searched her face impatiently, looking as though he were weighing the alternatives.

"I think you know very well that Pellea sent me," he said tersely.

He was right on that one. Pellea, the queen of the new, restored Ambrian monarchy, wanted her old best friend to come home to the castle for some reason. But she didn't seem to understand that it could never be home to Kim again. Her people, the Granvillis, had been driven out. The DeAngelis royals were in charge. There was no place for her there.

Still, Pellea didn't give up, and she kept sending people to try to lure Kim back. If she'd understood how deeply Kim's feelings of pain ran, if she had a clue how she resented the way she was treated toward the end, she might not have bothered.

Kim stared at the dark man and shook her head. She didn't have a lot of choice. She could stand here and scream at the top of her lungs, but he'd been right about the police. Since the end of the war, they were hard to find. Street crime was rampant. He could knock her on the head and drag her off into an alley before anyone even noticed, and from the look in his eyes, she had no doubt he wouldn't hesitate.

On the other hand, she could go with him to the coffee shop. It was a public place. He wouldn't do anything to her there. He could tell her his information, she could tell him why she didn't care, and hopefully, that would be that.

"All right," she said reluctantly. "Let's get this over with as quickly as possible."

His wide mouth twisted with a sort of mocking amusement at her words.

"Hold on a moment," he said, letting go of her arm and turning to snap a chain and lock on an ancient, crumbling motorcycle she hadn't noticed before, fastening it to the bus bench.

So that was how he'd caught her. She sighed, rocking on her heels, tempted to make a run for it now, while she had the opening—sort of—but just curious enough to give him a chance, at least for a few minutes.

Turning back, he tucked her hand into the crook of his arm in a familiar way she found utterly offensive, and escorted her into the coffee shop as though they made a habit of meeting this way.

She pulled her hand away as soon as she was able and slipped into a booth. He slid in across from her, holding her gaze with his own icy eyes. She stared back, feeling warmth begin to creep up her neck to her cheeks.

Why were his eyes so filled with accusations?

The coffee shop wasn't much at this point, but it had obviously been a trendy meeting place before the war. The remnants of the decor were still in place, looking shabby and worn, but still hopeful. A young girl who looked like she should have been home finishing up an assignment for her biology class came to take their order. She watched them brightly, her hair pulled into braids at either side of her head, and Kim smiled at her.

"I'll have a cup of tea," she said. "Herbal."

"Black coffee," he ground out. "Bold."

The girl nodded. "Nothing to eat?" she asked hopefully. "We have a lovely apple pie. The cook just took it out of the oven."

Now that she'd mentioned it, the scent of the pie was in the air. Kim breathed it in with pleasure, then caught the dark man's gaze and saw that he was doing the same thing.

Her eyes widened.

His narrowed.

Something electric snapped between them, shocking her. She wasn't sure if it was a sign of attraction or one of pure loathing and she looked away quickly, trying hard not to react.

But her heart pulsed. Was it fear? She didn't think so. But if not that...what?

She didn't even notice that he'd ordered them a piece of pie with vanilla ice cream and two forks until it appeared on the table along with their drinks.

That was just a little too friendly, wasn't it?

She looked up and met his gaze again. He was watching to see how she would react, and she flushed, looking back down. She thought about refusing to take a bite, but she knew that would seem churlish, and it did smell so good. She hadn't eaten all day. Could he hear her stomach rumble?

She looked at the luscious piece of pie. Steam was coming off the apples. The crust looked crisp and crumbling. The ice cream was just starting to melt around it.

Maybe just one bite. Or two.

They ate in silence. He very carefully only took his share and she wondered why. It was his pie, after all. She risked another glance at his face but his cold expression didn't tell her anything.

When every bit of pie was gone, he sighed with satisfaction and murmured, "That has got to be the best apple pie I've had since…"

He didn't go on and his mouth tightened. She wondered what painful memory had stopped him. So there was more to him than pure anger. That did make him seem a little more human.

The little café was warm. She opened her coat a bit, flushing as she noticed him looking at her nurse's uniform. She wasn't really a nurse, she just played one at the hospital, since actual nurses were in such short supply these days. But the uniform seemed to give people confidence.

"Tell me something," she said, looking at him directly. "Who are you?"

He took a deep breath before he answered. "I'm Jake Marallis. Pellea is my sister."

"Your sister!" She stared at him, surprised and not sure she believed him. "That's impossible. I've known Pellea all my life. She doesn't have a brother."

"Half brother." He shrugged. "My mother was married to her father before her mother was."

She thought that over quickly. It was possible, she supposed. But she knew she'd never seen him. Had Pellea ever mentioned him? Actually, now that she thought about it, she might have. She seemed to remember something.…

"You never lived in the castle?"

"No. Not in the old days."

She studied his face. Yes, she could see it now. That was what was so familiar about him. The look in his eyes was just like Pellea's, even though his eyes were blue and hers were dark. How extraordinary.

"You know she wants you to come home." He said it

softly, as though testing the waters. And he got a quick reaction.

"Home!" She winced, looking inside, probing her own response. Did it still hurt as badly as it used to? Was the feeling of betrayal healing over yet? Not a chance.

"That castle will never be home to me again."

But to her surprise, her tone came out more wistful than angry. She frowned. Maybe she *was* softening. She would have to keep an eye on that.

He leaned back, his narrow gaze penetrating without a hint of sympathy.

"What keeps you away, Kimmee?"

She grimaced. It had been a long time since anyone had called her by that childhood nickname. "It's Kim now, not Kimmee. That name is from my old life."

He shrugged. "As you wish." He raised one dark eyebrow. "The question still stands. I know I'm not the first my sister has sent to find you. Why won't you come back?"

It was none of his business, and he probably only wanted to know so that he could use the information against her, but for some reason, she found herself telling him anyway.

"Come back to what?" she said. "I've lived my whole life as part of the Granvilli era. I've never been a subject of the DeAngelis monarchy. I never backed the invasion. Ambria has been torn apart by the war between these two factions. The DeAngelis royalty now has the castle in their possession." She lifted her chin and met his gaze defiantly. "Well, bully for them. I'm with the Granvillis. And I won't turn traitor and go back to the protection of the castle just to have an easier life."

He frowned as though he were trying to understand but couldn't quite get there.

"And yet, from what I've heard, you helped Pellea hide the DeAngelis crown prince in her chambers, nurturing their relationship. How does that fit into the picture?"

She flushed. How did one go about explaining all the regrets in one's life?

"I'm a romantic at heart. What can I say?" She shrugged. "It seemed like the thing to do at the time." She shook her head, looking off into the distance, and added softly, "Who knew it would start a war?"

He didn't speak for a long moment, watching her. Finally she drew her thoughts back to the present and looked at him again. He was taking a long sip of his hot coffee. She made a face.

"I see you're planning to stay up all night tonight," she said tartly.

"Not really. Caffeine rarely bothers me."

Too cold blooded, she guessed.

"Does anything bother you?"

His eyes flashed. "Oh yes, Kim. A great deal bothers me."

She leaned toward him, curious. "Like what?"

He looked at her, seeming to see more deeply into her eyes than people usually did. She pulled back again, uncomfortable at the scrutiny, but he shook his head.

"This conversation isn't about me."

She shrugged. "I'm just trying to figure you out." She pressed her lips together, frowning at him with narrowed eyes. "Are you the enforcer? Are you supposed to get a little rough with me? Maybe even apply a few caveman tactics?"

His gaze was as frosty as ever, and completely impenetrable. His mouth twisted but he didn't deign to answer her charge. Her heart began to thump in her chest. He wasn't denying it. Just how far was he prepared to go? She hoped she wouldn't have to find out.

"Did Pellea send you as a last resort?" She leaned forward again, staring into his eyes and adding coolly, "Are you really as mean as you look?"

His eyes flickered with a flash of surprise, which he quickly quelled. "I prefer the term *professional*," he muttered crisply.

Her eyes widened. "As in professional hit man?" she whispered.

His handsome face registered a quick sense of outrage, colored by a hint of disbelief. "Oh, for God's sake..."

"No." She put up a hand as though to stop him. "I don't think I'm being ridiculous. Pellea seems to be relentless. Why shouldn't her emissary be the same?"

He felt insulted by her charge, that much was plain. "I like to think I'm a reasonable man with logic on my side," he said through gritted teeth. His gaze narrowed. "I'm hoping to avoid strong-arm tactics."

"Oh. How comforting."

He looked as though he would like to give her a good shake, but he controlled himself. "Let's get back to the point."

She could tell her eyes were sparkling at him. She was actually enjoying this in a way. He'd started out thinking he could bully her, and now she had him tied up in conversation not of his own making. Ha!

She sparkled at him some more. "Back to things that bother you. I'll bet you hate all of my favorite things."

He was beginning to look bewildered. "I don't know what you're talking about."

"Let's give it a try. How about these?" She pretended to be thinking. "Snowflakes on noses and whiskers on kittens."

A shadow flitted through his gaze and she couldn't tell if he was annoyed or amused.

"It's raindrops on roses," he said in a growl. "And why would they bother me?"

"I don't know."

She hid her amusement carefully, though she knew her eyes were a dead giveaway. He'd admitted he knew those lyrics and that just made her want to laugh out loud.

"You just seem like a bit of a Grinch. On the surface, I mean."

A look flashed on his face that surprised her. She'd hit a nerve. Or something. But he covered it up quickly enough.

"The fact is, I like whiskers on kittens as much as the next man," he said gruffly.

"Which means not a whole lot." She gave him a cynical look.

He threw out a hand as though asking for a witness to her nonsensical talk. "So now you're anti-men?"

"Not really." She shook her head. "Just mean men."

"I'm not mean." He glanced up quickly, realizing others could hear his raised voice, and he moderated his tone as he looked her in the eye, and then forced himself to relax. "Okay, so maybe I'm a little…hard. A little serious."

He appeared uncomfortable with the topic and she hid a smile. It was pretty obvious he wasn't used to letting the conversation go off on a tangent he hadn't initiated.

"Just another way of saying mean," she said, just to

needle him. "I'll bet you've never made a superfluous gesture of pure romance in your life."

"I..." He stopped himself, swearing softly and shaking his head as he looked at her with exasperation. "How the hell did we start down this road?"

She shrugged. "Just saying."

"Back to the subject. Again."

She looked innocent. "And that is?"

"You." He leaned back, pinning her with his intense gaze. "Going back to the castle. Reuniting with your family."

"My family." She grimaced. "And who might that be?"

The anger was back in his eyes, the accusations. A chill went down her spine. She knew something was coming, something she wasn't going to like.

"Are you still with Leonardo?" he asked, his voice low and menacing.

The name made her jump, and she blinked rapidly. She hadn't expected that one.

Leonardo Granvilli was the current leader of the rebel regime which had ruled the island nation of Ambria for over twenty-five years. He and his forces had only recently lost their power when the DeAngelis royal family retook most of the island, leaving the Granvilli faction a small section to the north, including the mountain city of Tantarette, where Jake had found her. Here was where the remnants of the Granvilli army and the civilian refugees had gathered, their dreams of glory ground to dust.

"Leonardo?" she asked, stalling for time. "Why would I be with Leonardo?"

His lip curled. "Because he fathered your baby."

She swallowed hard. She hadn't realized that was

common knowledge. "You don't know what you're talking about," she told him, her voice ringing with confidence even though her fingers trembled.

"I know enough."

"Do you actually know Leonardo?" she asked quickly, before he could say anything else. "I mean, have you personally talked to him?"

"Yes."

She studied his eyes. They were cold as a winter's day on the river. That thread of fear she'd thought she'd conquered was back.

"They say to know him is to love him," she said softly, just probing a bit.

His eyes flashed one unguarded spark of anger and his lip curled. "They lie."

She almost gave a nervous smile. They could certainly agree on that, but she wasn't going to tell him so.

She glanced around the café. Except for one man sipping soup by the window and an elderly couple just finishing up their meal, they were the only ones in the place.

"Aren't you afraid of being recognized? You're on the wrong side of the boundary line."

"No one knows me here. I never spent much time in Ambria before the war."

"A stranger in a strange land," she murmured.

"There's only one person I know well over here," he said, watching her eyes. "Leonardo Granvilli. He and I have a history that goes way back."

Her mouth went dry. There was something chilling in the way he'd said that. She tried to remember if Leonardo had ever mentioned Pellea having a brother, but she couldn't come up with a thing. It wasn't that she didn't believe him. It was more that she hoped he was lying so she wouldn't have to care.

She glanced down at the empty plate the pie had come on. The waitress hadn't been back to take it away. She had a twinge of nostalgia for the few moments when they had first arrived, when it almost seemed they might be able to have a normal chat. That was gone now. The sense of his leashed antagonism was palpable. He despised her. She had to get away from him.

"Listen, we're wasting time," he said bluntly. "Here's the deal. I'm taking you back. Pellea needs you and I promised her I wouldn't come back without you."

The man was direct. Painfully so. There was no warmth, no humanity to him. Except for the superficial likeness, she could see nothing of Pellea there.

She shook her head as he spoke. "No."

"You have no choice any longer. The game's up, Kimmee—or Kim, as you prefer. Everyone knows the truth now about who you really are. It's your duty to come back."

"Who I really am?" She stared at him blankly. "What are you talking about?"

His mouth twitched impatiently. "The last messenger Pellea sent must have given you a hint. You're a DeAngelis. The youngest of your generation. Last of the royal babies. Sister to Monte and all the rest."

For a moment, she thought she'd heard him wrong. Then she wondered if he were joking. Finally, as the look in his face and the tone of his voice began to sink in, she realized he really meant what he was saying.

And suddenly, she felt as though she couldn't breathe, and would probably never be able to breathe again.

This couldn't be happening. It was too bizarre. But

she knew she had heard something like this before. The last one who'd come looking for her had babbled the same words, but she hadn't paid any attention. She knew they would do anything, say anything, to get her to come back, and she hadn't bought into it. She knew who her mother was. She'd been born in the castle to Queen Elineas's favorite lady-in-waiting a week before the Granvillis overthrew the DeAngelis monarchy. Everyone knew that.

Didn't they?

But where that last messenger had been easy to dismiss, this one wasn't. He didn't seem like a man who did much kidding around.

She shook her head harder, feeling sick. "No. Someone made that up. There's no truth to it. It's ridiculous."

He gave her an incredulous look. "Are you trying to tell me you're ready to reject a place in the royal family? Are you really that reckless?"

She was trembling. Her teeth began to chatter. He was telling her what he believed to be the truth. She could see it in his eyes. But it couldn't be true. To believe what he was saying would be to smash everything she'd depended on as reality for her whole life. It was too much.

"It can't be done, Kim. Once you're royal, you're royal. It's a very exclusive club, but you can't resign from it. There's no opting out. You're stuck with it."

She put her hand over her mouth and started to slide out of the booth. "I…I'm going to be sick," she mumbled to him as she hurried toward the bathroom.

He watched her go, then shook his head and picked up his coffee mug, draining the last of it.

And that was why it took him a moment to realize

something wasn't adding up. He frowned, turned his head, and uttered a very ugly oath as he leaped to his feet.

Kim hadn't made it into the bathroom. Obviously, that had never been her destination. Instead, she'd headed out the door and was now running as fast as she could for home.

CHAPTER TWO

KIM ran down the alley and then cut in to take a short cut through a vacant lot. She hadn't lived in that area long but she had taken Dede on enough baby carriage rides through the neighborhood to know a thing or two. She was running hard, but carefully. The snow was coming down harder and there were patches of black ice. She didn't want to slip.

Her heart was thumping in her throat and the air stung her lungs. Whatever she did, she couldn't lead him back to the building where her rooms were.

Jake Marallis terrified her. The others had been easy to brush off. He had no intention of being brushed. He had the cool, clear gaze of a man who thought he knew the truth, and that was one of the scariest things in the universe. He was hard. He was unrelenting. And that was why she had to make sure he never found her again.

The things he had told her were jarring, even chilling, and definitely uncomfortable. She didn't want to believe them. She wasn't going to believe them. Why should she? And even if they were true, she didn't want to do anything about it.

"Just leave me alone," she moaned to herself as she ran. She doubled back, finding another alley that he would never see in time. She headed away from the main street, hoping to lose him in the tangle of tiny dead-end lanes.

Then she would double back, grab Dede and go.

Go where? That was a question she couldn't deal with just yet.

She planned to go in the back entrance of her building, but only once she'd made sure he wasn't right behind her. Then she would take the stairs up to her rooms, being careful not to turn on any lights that might catch his attention, and she would pay the babysitter to stay on for an hour or so more, just to make sure he didn't see her leave. Yes, that was it. If she was very cautious, it should work.

She'd been running so hard, she couldn't breathe. She had to stop, leaning against a building, to catch her breath so she could make the final race count. For the first moment, she couldn't hear anything but her own ragged breathing. But as her breath caught up, she heard something else. Someone else was running across pavement. It had to be him.

Panic flared in her chest and she took off again. Her building was just ahead. She'd barely rounded the last corner when she heard a terrible sound, stopping her in her tracks. A car was skidding, probably on an icy patch. There was a crash, metal on stone, and then someone cried out. She heard the car backing up, then racing off, metal falling from it as it went. But there was no more sound of running feet.

She stood very still, holding her breath and saying a little prayer. "Please, no, don't let it be that."

A male voice groaned in the distance and her heart sank. It looked like her prayer had not been answered. There was a very good chance that Jake had been hit by a skidding car.

What now?

She listened for another few seconds. Would another car stop? Would someone run to his rescue? But she didn't hear any more cars. The whole area had an eerie silence to it, like a ghost town, as though the snow were blanketing all evidence of human activity. There was no one there…no one to come to his aid.

She stood very still, but her mind worked frantically. Could she leave him there? Could she run on home and try to find a phone and make an anonymous call to the police? Or the hospital? Could she really do that? How long would it be before they finally came to find him?

All night, probably.

She heard something else, like metal being moved, and then a gasp, as though he were trying to get up and was in pain. She looked around at the darkened buildings. Didn't anyone hear him? Wasn't anyone going to run down to see what had happened?

By now she was almost sure it was Jake. And he was hurt. Really hurt.

And she knew, heart sinking, that she couldn't just leave him. She was scared to death of the man, but she couldn't let him lie in the street after being hit by a car. She had to go back. He was Pellea's brother. She would have to deal with the consequences later.

She waited another moment, hoping against hope that she would hear someone going to see about him. But there was no one. She was going to have to do it.

Taking a deep breath, she turned and hurried toward where the noise had been coming from.

She saw him right away. He'd pulled himself out of the street and up onto the curb, but he looked in bad shape. There was a bloody scrape across the whole left side of his face and the set of his left leg looked awkward. As she reached him, he looked up with hugely dilated eyes and didn't seem to recognize who she was.

"I…the car…."

"Hush," she said, holding back her own anxiety. "Let me take a look."

She was no medical professional but she had been working part-time as a nurse's aide at the hospital, both here and at her usual home by the shore. She'd seen more broken and wounded men from the war than she would have ever hoped to see in her lifetime, and she had some idea of what to look for.

Though his leg looked oddly askew, she was pretty sure his bones weren't broken, at least not in an obvious way. She was more worried about his groggy behavior. He still didn't seem to know her. After a quick examination, she sat back and looked at him. Now what?

One thing was certain—she couldn't just leave him here in the street. That whole running away and hiding from him scenario was by the boards.

On the other hand, he was hurt and it wouldn't be so easy for him to force her to do what he wanted now. Was it really the balanced situation she was presenting herself with? Maybe, maybe not. But she knew, as long as he could make it, she was going to take him to her apartment. What else could she do?

"Come on," she said, helping him up as he grimaced painfully, favoring the crooked leg and gasping as they began to move. "Lean on me. I'm going to take you home."

It took longer than she'd expected, but she managed to maneuver him into the elevator and take him up to her third floor set of rooms. She tried to ignore the blood he was dripping from a gash in his chin. Hopefully she would be able to get back and clean it all up later. Trying to take up as much of his weight as she could, she got him to the door of her apartment, and then inside and onto the couch.

Kristi, the babysitter, was surprised, but Kim quickly paid her off and sent her home. And then she stood and stared at the long, lean man who had dropped into the center of her life.

Dede was asleep. Jake was awake, but not really coherent. She was worried that he might have been hit harder than she'd thought at first. Reaching out, she felt his forehead. Cold and clammy. From the little she knew about such things, she didn't think that was good.

She looked down at his stark, handsome face, and her stomach did a little somersault dance. She was afraid of the man, and yet there was something so compelling about his dark, brooding looks, even with the injuries. She bit her lip and wondered if this was how some women ended up with men who were all wrong for them.

"Taking home strays," she murmured, shaking her head. "It'll come back to bite you every time."

That made her laugh a bit. If anyone was the stray here, it was her. He was a thoroughbred, through and through. Looks like that were never deceiving.

She knew very well there was no point in trying to make a call for a doctor or the hospital. The war had done its damage to modern communications on the island. The few cell phone towers they'd once had were bombed during the fighting and what land lines anyone had left rarely worked.

And even if you could get through, medical help was in short supply these days. You were lucky if you could find a physician even at the hospital where she worked.

The most competent ones had left for the winning side of the war long since, and the ones who'd stayed were haggard with overwork.

Unless she could think of some miracle, fast, she was on her own.

She did the best she could cleaning him up. Dede woke up and fussed a bit, so she alternated between her baby and the vagabond she'd brought home. Soaking a clean cloth in cool water, she wiped the blood from the scrapes across his face, then dabbed at them with hydrogen peroxide, working carefully around the gash on his chin.

He was in pain but he'd lost the grogginess that she was pretty sure must have come from shock. By the time she finished cleaning his face, he was pretty aware of what was going on.

"My leg," he muttered as she tried to cover the scrapes with gauze and bandages. "What the hell's wrong with my leg?"

"I don't know," she said. "Is that the only place that hurts? I mean really seriously?"

He looked up at her and for once, his eyes focused. He knew who she was. "Maybe we should start by mentioning areas that don't hurt," he muttered. "That wouldn't take as long."

That did it. She would have to do something. It was truly amazing how her attitude toward him could change in such a short time, but to see this large, strong and forceful man in pain and so vulnerable touched something deep inside. It made her just a little bit crazy. She had to take care of him.

"I'm going to try to get you some help," she told him. "I'm going to try to find a way to call the hospital…"

"No." His eyes were burning and he grabbed her

hand. "You can't do that. You know I'm not here le-gally. They'll throw me in jail."

"Oh." She hadn't thought of that. She looked at the way he was holding her hand, as though it were a life-line. Still, that he'd told her not to contact the hospital was telling. Despite his weakened state, he still ordered her about, not asked politely.

"I…I guess I'll see if I can find some pain killers at least," she said, using her other hand to peel away his fingers and wrest herself free.

He nodded, closing his eyes and wincing. "That would be good," he whispered.

She took a deep breath and considered the options.

What would she do with this beautiful, damaged man? An expert really needed to take a look and make sure nothing extreme had happened to him. She had no idea how to check for internal bleeding or broken ribs or anything major like that. Just the thought that he might be badly hurt and not showing it made her heart begin to race again. If you didn't treat that sort of injury, bad things could happen. She felt a deep sense of urgency to do something.

There was one source of hope she could think of. She didn't know many people who lived in this build-ing. She'd only been here a little over a month herself. But she did know one, and she'd consulted him before when her baby's problems had scared her enough to seek help. She just didn't know how useful he would be at this time of night.

The lucky part was, he'd once been a physician. The unlucky part—he was a pretty heavy-duty alcoholic. The word was, he'd lost his license to practice medi-cine because of that. But if you caught Dr. Harve at a good time, he could be very helpful.

Tonight, he seemed only mildly sloshed.

"Of course I'll come and take a look at your young man," he said jovially when she knocked on his door. "What are neighbors for?"

She went back to prepare Jake, pulling off his leather coat and shirt and loosening his jeans. He was conscious and he pushed her away.

"Your leg," she said urgently. "We're going to have to take off your pants one way or another."

He shook his head and she didn't know if he was being modest or if his brain was addled with the pain.

"I work at the hospital, you know," she grumbled as she grabbed a pair of strong scissors and began to cut open the denim cloth that encased the bad leg. "I've done this before."

He didn't protest again, but he groaned in a way that chilled her.

"I've got a real doctor coming," she reassured him. "He'll be here any minute. He's been a big help with my baby's problems. He's even searching for a specialist for me to take her to. You'll like him, I'm sure."

She felt like she was babbling, but it was mostly to try to keep him calm and to prepare him for what the doctor was going to have to do. There was more pain coming, she was sure.

Dr. Harve came in, cracking jokes and exuding a certain brand of warmth that probably worked with most of his patients. It was his rapid diagnosis that Jake's knee was badly wrenched and seriously dislocated, and he spent some time treating it, chatting through the whole thing. He elicited a few smothered yells of pain and a lot of writhing from Jake as he manipulated the joint, but he talked right over them all. Meanwhile, Kim closed her eyes and covered her ears and moaned softly in sympathy.

"The connective tissue will be sore for a while," he told her as he began the final wrap. "And it will be a few weeks before he will want to run any marathons. But he'll be okay soon enough."

"What about the rest of him?" she asked anxiously.

"I'd say he was lucky he was wearing that leather coat," he said, nodding toward where it lay in the corner. "Otherwise he'd be a lot more scraped up. As it is, he's got a few cracked ribs. He'll want to be careful of those, but the pain will definitely remind him of that. I can wrap his chest, but you can't do much else for ribs. You might want to watch for signs of concussion. I don't see any evidence of internal bleeding, but if you see anything strange, don't hesitate to come on over and tell me about it."

She nodded, watching him work. This was all a bit surreal. Just an hour ago she'd been running from this man, running for her life. Now she was trying hard to help him.

"What about that deep gash on his chin? It's still bleeding."

"Yes, I've been looking at that." He sighed. "You know, ordinarily I would probably give him a few stitches. But the way my hands are shaking tonight..." He held them up for her to see and didn't finish the sentence.

He didn't have to. She was amazed he was able to do as well as he had been.

He cocked an eyebrow her way. "I don't suppose you...?"

"Oh no," she said quickly. "I wouldn't trust myself."

He nodded sadly. "Don't worry. We're not going to

ruin his pretty face too badly here. I've got some good butterfly bandages that will do almost as well."

She noticed, with a slight jolt, that Jake's eyes were open and looking directly into hers. The doctor kept on talking while he worked on the bloody chin, but she and Jake seemed to be locked in a gaze neither one could tear away from. Her pulse was racing. What was he thinking? Was he trying to tell her there was going to be a pause, but no escape for her? That he knew all he needed to know about her now? That he had her trapped?

"Okay, my dear, if you would hand me my bag, I think I'll give this fellow something to help him sleep for a while so he can begin to heal."

She finally pulled her gaze away and took a deep breath, getting him his bag and trying to calm her pulse. She didn't ask where he got his drugs, she was just grateful he had some. She was sure he must have a connection with the usual black market sources. Since the war, that was the way most people got anything important. The usual supply lines were completely cut off.

She knew he wasn't supposed to call himself a doctor, but he'd been a godsend to her for the six weeks or so she'd lived here. He'd helped her with Dede's problems many times, and he'd promised to try to find a real pediatrician for her. Baby doctors seemed to have been the first things the country had run out of once the war began.

Dede started to cry in earnest and Dr. Harve laughed, looking at her. "You decided taking care of one patient wasn't enough so you added a new guy," he noted, grinning at her. "Some people are just gluttons for punishment."

The "new guy" isn't going to stay beyond the night,

she thought to herself, gearing up to be tough if she had to. *At least, I hope not.*

Dr. Harve was finishing up and he sidled closer to her and asked softly, "So who is this guy, anyway? Are you going to be okay with him here?"

She looked up in surprise. Was the latent hostility between the two of them so obvious? For just a moment, she wondered if she should tell him not to mention Jake's presence to anyone else in the building. But that would only raise new red flags. And anyway, Kristi, the babysitter, had seen him, too. It was a bit late for secrecy.

"Don't worry," she told him quickly. "He's...the brother of an old friend. I'll be fine."

He shrugged, his eyes glinting with a new, greedy light. "Well, I notice you're not calling the police to report the accident. So I figured...."

He gave her a look that made her think, for just a moment, that he might be shaking her down. But that couldn't be. The man was a doctor. Well, sort of. She looked at him more closely and he laughed, as though it had all been a joke, and went back to preparing to leave.

She got out some cash she had stashed in the closet, and gave it to him. She always paid him for his work and advice. That seemed to make him happier and he left as cheerfully as he'd come. She frowned, watching him go. What if he got in touch with the police himself? What would she do if the authorities suddenly appeared at the door?

She was harboring an illegal alien—someone connected to the highest reaches of the enemy's administration. No wonder the man was having thoughts of being paid for his silence. His whole mode of survival depended on grabbing a buck where he could.

She turned back into the apartment with a sigh. Sometimes she felt as though she lived in one of those fast-paced video games where there was danger all around and holes you could fall into and people ready to leap out at you with a mallet to the head. Where the heck was the Off switch?

She looked into the living room at her latest piece of dangerous baggage. Finally, she and Jake were going to be alone. Surely they would have to hash some of this over. She had butterflies as she came closer, looking at him tentatively, wondering how he would act. But his eyes were closed. She frowned, feeling strangely disappointed, as though she'd been ready for a fight and now it had been postponed. She went nearer.

"Jake, do you want some water? Or something else to drink?"

He didn't move. His eyelids didn't even flutter. He was out cold.

She had a lot of thinking to do, a lot of decisions to make, a bit of planning go over. But at least she had a little time now. He was in no condition to drag her off to the castle against her will. Whatever he'd planned to do couldn't be done in the next twenty-four hours. She was in a narrow safety zone.

She looked at him, so beautiful of body, so wounded and still. He had a lot of skin showing and a whole set of gorgeous golden muscles. She shivered, looking at him, and that made her realize she needed to make sure he didn't get a chill.

She went to get him a shawl and laid it gently around his shoulders, then began to tuck it in with her fingers. Her hands slipped over the hard, rounded muscles in his shoulders and she gasped at the sensation that rippled through her. Her face was getting hot.

"Ohmigosh," she moaned. "Stop it!"

Closing her eyes, she bit down hard on her lower lip, willing the delicious feelings that set off the man-woman thing to go away. She counted to ten before she opened them again. Then she turned away, not daring to look at him until her blood had stopped racing through her veins.

Leaning against the sink in her makeshift kitchen, she tried some deep breathing. She couldn't let this happen. She was not going to respond in a sensual way to this man who hated her.

And then there was the question of why he hated her. It had been a mystery to her until he'd mentioned Leonardo. The disgust in his voice, the flare in his eyes, told her the cause would probably not be a surprise after all. It seemed her relationship with Leonardo was enough to convince him she wasn't much good.

She wondered fleetingly what Leonardo could have done to him to bring on this antagonism, but that was a useless exercise to pursue. Leonardo had done something to just about everybody, one way or another. If you lived in Ambria, it was just a matter of time before Leonardo insulted your life in some way.

But she could never forget that he was Dede's father. So having him killed was out of the question. She shrugged, resigned to the vicissitudes of fate—for now.

Jake woke up with a start, not sure where he was. The baby was crying. Somebody should go to the baby.

Where was Cyrisse?

He pulled himself up, blinking hard to get the sleep out of his eyes. He was stiff, sore, miserable. Baby still crying. His leg hurt, and so did his head, but the baby was crying. He looked around, dazed. Someone had to take care of the baby.

"Cyrisse?" he said.

And then the familiar big black hole opened up inside him and he remembered. There was no baby. The baby was gone. And so was Cyrisse. He lost his balance and fell back onto the pillows, overwhelmed by the pure evil of the black hole, the hopelessness, almost ready to give in and let it swallow him.

But there was still a baby crying. He made a major effort and roused himself again, looking for where the baby was.

The light was dim. He could hardly make out the furniture in the shabby apartment. What the hell? He'd never been in this place before. How had he got here?

And he began to remember.

Kimmee.

Running.

The car.

Pain.

Was this Kimmee's baby? He pulled himself up high enough to see where the crib was. A baby was crying alright, but it was Leonardo's.

Leonardo's baby. Anger swirled in his dazed brain. In some societies it would be expected that he would take Leonardo's baby if he had the chance—as Leonardo had taken his. He'd vowed he would make that bastard pay. What was stopping him now?

Slowly, painfully, he rose to his feet, keeping his weight all on his right side. Grimacing, he began to hobble toward the crib, using various pieces of furniture along the way as a crutch. A wave of nausea came over him. He stopped, waiting for it to pass. Two more steps and he was looking down into the baby's crib.

The tot looked up at him in surprise, eyes huge in the dim light. She looked about nine months old and she wasn't crying anymore, but she made a curious noise. It sounded like a question to him, like, "Who the heck are you?"

He stared down at her. She was Leonardo's but that didn't seem to penetrate. She was a baby. Who on earth could hurt a baby? Not him. He gave her one last look and then he turned to go back.

But she started crying again.

He stood there for a moment, trying to keep his balance and at the same time, trying to make sense of this. Leonardo's baby. So what?

But it was also Kimmee's. A baby was a baby, and this one needed help. Muttering to himself, he turned back, scooped her up and brought her to his chest. And let out a quick scream of pain that almost knocked him off his feet. The baby began to slip through his hands, falling headfirst toward the floor.

"No!"

He grabbed her just in time and clung to her, holding her high enough to avoid the damaged area that was his chest, but still gasping from the pain.

The baby cried harder.

"Okay, kid," he said gruffly. "You gotta stop the crying. It's like a hammer against my head. Come on." He rocked her, wincing as he experimented until he found just how close he could go to the ribs. "Come on."

He started back toward the couch, then took a turn as he noticed the overstuffed rocking chair.

"Here we go," he told the sweet little child. "Come on, now. Let's get some sleep."

Slouching carefully into the chair, he began to rock. The baby quieted almost instantly. He tried a little humming to hurry the process along, but it hurt and he had to stop. His eyes closed. The baby slipped down to a comfortable place between his chest and his upper arm.

They both slept.

Kim was in heaven. For once, there was hot water and she was going to make the most of it. She stood in the shower and let the silvery warmth crash over her. Wonderful.

For just a moment she could forget that she'd brought her biggest current enemy into this house and let him sleep very close to her baby girl. She could forget how difficult and frustrating work at the hospital was, how worried she was about Dede, how scared Jake made her—and just exist in the wet and the warm. She even began to sing an old Cole Porter tune, just to prove how happy she was in the moment.

But suddenly, she heard something. She couldn't be certain what it was. Quickly, she turned off the water and listened hard. Nothing. She must have been imagining it. Sighing, she turned the water back on. In this building, you had to grab the good before someone came and took it away from you. She was going to shower like there was no tomorrow. And for all she knew, maybe there wasn't.

Ten minutes later she turned off the water again and slipped out of the shower, luxuriating in a large, fluffy towel. She patted down her wet hair and rubbed on some cream and sang softly to herself. For the moment, she was happy.

Slipping into her warm nightgown, she hung the towel on the hook and started out into the living room.

The first place she looked was in Dede's crib. And it was empty.

A scream began to shove its way up her throat. Panic clutched at her chest, her heart, her mind. She couldn't breathe. Turning quickly, she saw Jake in the rocking chair, Dede clutched up between his arm and his chest, and the panic left her body like air out of a spent balloon. She crumpled to the floor in front of the rocking chair and stared up at the two of them. Relief chased chagrin through her heart.

"Thank you, thank you," she prayed softly.

They looked so peaceful, both of them totally captured by sleep. Jake's face, with its gauze bandage over the chin, looked almost benign. And Dede had relaxed completely in his arms, her little face untroubled by the pain she suffered from so often.

Watching them, tears began to fill her eyes and then spill down her cheeks. She tried to wipe them away, but they just came faster.

It was the release, she told herself. The relief of knowing she had a few hours when she wasn't going to worry about how she was going to get away from Jake and avoid going back to face the DeAngelis royals, relief in knowing someone else was here to help her with Dede if she had one of her spasms. Relief in just having another adult here with her.

Most of the time it all seemed to be on her shoulders. For just a moment, she would let the burden fall away and let herself cry.

CHAPTER THREE

Morning had come. Jake could feel the difference without even opening his eyes. Kim was murmuring to her baby and getting delightful gurgles in return.

Baby laughter was a beautiful sound. He longed for the day when hearing it wouldn't cut him to the quick any longer.

He pushed that thought away. It did no good to dwell on heartache. And he was glad to hear Kim's baby sounding happy. It seemed to him there had been a few times during the night he'd heard something different from the little girl. Or maybe he'd been dreaming.

He sighed, not so sure whether he had finally rejoined the real world and left his nightmares behind. He'd been in and out of consciousness and the hours had blended together pointlessly. For all he knew, it could be days later by the time he'd begun to regain full use of his groggy brain. Days, or maybe hours.

Now Kim was moving around the room, gathering things up. He cracked his eyes open only enough to see her standing in front of the window. Morning light was streaking in, outlining her in silhouette, showing off every curve of her lovely form beneath the lacy nightgown she wore. The power of that image stunned him like a sucker punch to the gut. The woman appealed to his senses, there was no denying that.

But only physically, he told himself quickly, closing his eyes tightly again. He despised everything she stood for.

He tried to go over what had happened in the past twelve hours, how he'd ended up here like this. His mind was fairly clear. He pretty much knew where he was and why he was here. But that didn't stop him from resenting it.

"Are you awake?" she asked him.

He opened one eye and looked at her. She was still in the damn nightgown. He closed it again.

"No," he said gruffly.

"Yes, you are." She bent over where he still half-sat, half-lay in the overstuffed rocking chair he seemed to have slept in. He felt her cool hand on his forehead and he frowned, pulling away from her touch.

"How do you feel?"

He opened his eyes again. She was too close to avoid. Her brown eyes looked sleepy but concerned. Blond hair flew around her face in disarray. She looked like a woman who had just risen from her bed, which he supposed was exactly what she was. There was no getting away from it. He was going to have to get used to watching her bounce around in a gauzy shift he could practically see through even without the backlighting.

Fate worse than death, he supposed, laughing at himself. The horror. He drew in a deep breath, suddenly feeling as though he had warm butterscotch flowing through his veins. Swallowing hard, he tried to avoid looking at her.

"I feel like I just got run over by a truck," he said, sounding grumpy. "What do I look like?"

She nodded. "That, too. It's pretty much what happened."

He nodded and gingerly touched the bandage on his chin. "Is it?" he muttered, then looked at her more sharply. "Okay, you want to tell me what exactly happened last night? How much did you see?"

"I didn't see you get hit but..."

"Whoa, slow down." He held up a hand, frowning as he went over the events of the last evening in his head. "Let's start at the beginning." He fixed her with an intense look. "We were sitting there in the café. You implied you were heading for the bathroom. Somehow you got diverted."

She nodded, dropping onto the arm of the couch nearest too him. "I saw it a little differently. We were sitting there in the café and you began to threaten me."

He looked up at her, frowning. That wasn't the way he remembered it at all. "What?"

She shrugged. "You said you were taking me back to the castle."

"That was a threat?" He made a face, wondering why women were so often so unreasonable. "I considered it a promise, not a threat."

"Then you claimed I was really a DeAngelis." Her look was full of skepticism, as though she was pretty sure he'd made it up. "I guess you thought that gave you permission to force me to go back. And I decided you were obviously a raving lunatic and I had to get out of there."

"So you ran."

"I ran."

"And I ran after you."

"But you didn't catch me." Her eyes sparkled.

"No, you're right there." He had to admit it, he'd been

off his game from the beginning and he hadn't realized she would be so hard to catch. "You were running all over the place."

"I didn't want to lead you right back here."

He looked at her, a slow sense of satisfaction taking over. "And yet, here I am."

She shrugged that away. She didn't want to concede the point. "I didn't see the accident, but from what I could hear, it sounded like a car skidded on ice and hit you."

"Hit and run?"

She nodded.

He searched her eyes, his own hooded. "Why didn't you just leave me there?"

"Please," she said, as though there had been no dilemma at all. "You're Pellea's brother."

And still, he wondered…. "So that's why you rescued me?"

"Pretty much." She gave him a look. "I can't think of any other reason."

He nodded slowly. He still didn't completely believe it. What was he supposed to think of this woman? Ever since he'd found out about her relationship with Leonardo, he's assumed she was bad news. If there really could be such a thing as a nemesis in life, that was what Leonardo was to him. The emotional side of him wanted the man dead. The more realistic side realized killing Leonardo would mean only bad things for himself. Was revenge worth destroying your life for? That was something he still had to think through.

"And you got me medical help without having me arrested," he added, grateful yet not sure how to express it without getting too friendly. "Pretty good work."

She favored him with a smile that lit up the room. "Every now and then I can be pretty terrific."

He drew back, disturbed by how pretty she could look at times. "I wouldn't go that far," he said grumpily.

"Whatever," she said lightly. "Dr. Harve seems to think you're not too badly hurt. You ought to be okay in a couple of days."

"Good." He frowned. "Hey, what kind of a doctor doesn't do stitches because his hands are shaking?"

She bit her lip. "You caught that, huh?"

"I did. What's the deal?"

She sighed. "Jake, you know it's almost impossible to find a real doctor these days. Besides the problem of you being here illegally."

"So what is he, a phony?"

"No, he's got real medical training. But he lost his license to practice at some point. I don't know what for."

He frowned. "So he's still practicing, but ineptly?"

"No. I think he did fine with you last night. But you might say he's illegal, just like you are. Only in a different realm."

"You might say that." His blue eyes were penetrating. "Or you might admit he's probably a quack. And that is something I'll never be."

She shook her head. "I just want you to be healed." She watched him closely as she added, "And then you can go back where you came from."

He looked up into her face. "Not without you. I told you that from the start."

She stared at him, all humor gone, eyes darkening. He blinked, thinking a cloud had come out to cover the sun. Had the air suddenly gone colder? She looked away and sighed, then looked back.

"If you're keeping tabs on me because you think I'll lead you to where Leonardo is, you're in for a big disappointment," she warned, just in case.

His blue eyes snapped and searched her face. "You and the leader of your country don't hang out much anymore, huh?"

She gave him a dark look, but no words in response.

"Doesn't he want to come see his baby?"

She stared at him, exasperated. He had some nerve with his nosy questions.

"See, that's what I don't get," he went on. "You've got the only baby Leonardo has ever been known to have fathered. Therefore, you've got the heir to the Granvilli empire, such as it is these days. And yet you're hiding in shabby rooms, desperately trying to locate a doctor for your child. It doesn't add up."

Did he think she had been with Leonardo to get what she could from him? That she was some sort of gold digger? Wow. If he only knew how far off the mark he really was.

"If you think anyone on this side of the island has any money, you'll have to think again. Even the Granvilli family. Losing a war makes you broke."

He nodded. He understood that. "Of course, they lost most of their holdings over the past year or so, but you never know. The South may rise again."

"Not in my lifetime." She glared at him. "And anyway, no one knows where Leonardo is."

"That's understandable," he said, his mouth twisted in something like a mocking smile. "If anyone knew where he was he'd probably be dead by now." He looked up and just caught the tail end of a grin leaving her face. "You smile at that. Now I'm completely confused." He shook his head.

"Don't be," she shot back at him. "People are complex. We all have different things that drive us. And anyway, you know darn well you would enjoy seeing him squirm yourself."

"I see," he said slowly, analyzing the situation as best he could. "You're angry that he's turned his back on you."

That would be the day. She rolled her eyes. "No, I'm angry that you keep bringing him up. I don't want to think about him. I don't want to hear his name. Please stop."

"Sure. Sorry." But he stared at her as though she was a puzzle he needed to solve.

She changed the subject. "Why did you pick up Dede last night when I was in the shower?" she asked softly.

"Is that your little girl's name?"

"Yes."

He shrugged. "She was crying. And that made me think about my own little girl."

He winced as he said it, immediately wishing he hadn't. He should have kept his thoughts to himself.

"You have a little girl?" she asked, face lightening.

He turned to look into her dark eyes and shook his head slowly. "Not anymore," he said, and then he looked away. He'd caught the beginning of her shocked look and he didn't want to see any more of it.

She touched him. Reaching out, she put her soft hand over his and leaned toward him. "I'm sorry," she whispered softly, and then she drew away again.

He looked at her. Her eyes were huge with sympathy for him. He didn't want any damn sympathy. But something in those eyes warmed him in a strange, sensual way. He had to admit, if he ever had to take sympathy from someone, hers would be the one he would want.

But that was a stupid thought. He turned away again. This was driving him crazy. He didn't want to like her. He didn't want to feel attracted. And if this kept up, he'd be tempted to do things he could only regret.

"Listen, do me a favor," he said hoarsely. "Could you go get some clothes on? Then maybe I can stop staring into corners in order to avoid looking at you."

"Oh. I'm sorry." But she laughed. He couldn't help but think an evil thread ran through that laugh. She knew the power she had over him, didn't she?

"Really, I'm not used to having a man around in the morning. I didn't think…."

Yeah, right. Women.

She put on jeans and a loose-fitting shirt and spent the next hour taking care of her baby. He didn't look over to see what she was doing. The drugs were still affecting him and he slipped in and out of sleep for what seemed like hours.

The next time he was awake, he could see that Kim was getting ready to go to work. The white nurse's uniform looked a little tight on her, as though she'd borrowed it from someone else—and maybe had washed it too often since. But the way it fit—short and snug—set off her deliciously curvy body to great advantage, at least from his perspective. Watching her move, he got a surge of a reminder that for all his injuries, he was a man and still had some male reactions after all. That almost made him smile.

"Okay," he said when she came close enough for conversation without shouting across the room. "When do we leave?"

Kim turned to stare at him. "I'm not going anywhere."

He tried to act sure of himself, but it was tough in

the state he found himself in. "Sure you are," he said as firmly as he could. "You're going back to the castle."

She stood over him, a slight, superior smile on her face, as though she couldn't believe he was even pretending he could manage any of this.

"I don't think you could follow through on that right now, even if you wanted to," she told him with a smirk.

He frowned at her and she gave him a mock frown back. "So you're Pellea's brother," she said, looking him over as though for the first time. Then she grinned. "Pellea and I grew up like sisters, you know. So that would almost make you my brother as well."

He gave her a look that told her she was so far off base, the moon was closer. "Not hardly," he said with startling emphasis. The fact that he found her sexually appealing was so obvious in the way he said it, it almost made her blush. But not quite.

"I think you're a big talker," she said. "But right now, you can't produce the follow-through." She glared at him. "I'm not going anywhere with you."

He held his own, but it wasn't easy. "I'm damaged, but not defeated. I'm ready to go, and you're going with me."

"Really? And how do you think we're going to make the trip? A magic carpet, maybe?"

"Hey, my motorcycle." His face changed as he remembered where he'd left it. "I wonder if it's still there."

"Chained to the bus bench? I doubt it."

He frowned, looking at her speculatively, but realizing right away she wasn't going to go get it for him. "It might be. No one's stolen it yet and I've had it for days."

She knew what he was thinking. "Forget it," she said.

"Besides, you only have the one cycle. We can't all go on that."

"Sure we can. It's a good old sturdy one. We could make it."

Her eyes opened wide in mock horror. She didn't believe a word of it. She knew he had to be kidding. If he was serious, he was certifiable.

"I see. You're planning to put Dede and me on the back of a motorcycle and go careening through the mountains." She glared at him. "Are you crazy?"

He sighed, realizing he was really too weak for this argument right now. His whole body was aching.

"Maybe I am," he admitted softly.

She rolled her eyes and turned away.

He flexed the muscles in his legs, wondering if he could trust them and deciding against trying. Not yet. Maybe the next time he was conscious. He closed his eyes, resigning himself to more sleep.

He woke some time later to find the doctor hovering over him, checking his eyes, then taking the gauze off the cut in his chin to make sure no infection was setting in. He talked the whole time but Jake only caught a few words here and there.

"You're probably sore all over," the doctor was saying now. "You got hit pretty hard. You're lucky you didn't break any bones."

"Tell me something I don't know," Jake muttered under his breath.

"What's that you say?"

Jake shook his head. He'd been talking to himself when you came right down to it.

"Where's Kim?" he managed to say aloud as he began to realize there didn't seem to be any sign of her.

"Kim? Oh, she had to go to work. She'll be back to-night."

Would she? A small part of his brain was signaling him with a warning. She might try to take off again. Why wouldn't she? But there really wasn't much he could do about it in his present state. The doctor was right. He had to heal fast.

"Where's the baby?" he asked.

"The babysitter took her over to her apartment," he said, and suddenly he looked shifty. "Say, what's your name anyway? In case I need to fill out any papers or anything."

Despite his condition, Jake recognized a phony cover-up when he heard one. "Jake Jonas," he lied, slurring his words and closing his eyes to forestall any more questions.

"Where are you from, Jake Jonas?"

Jake just shook his head.

The doctor hesitated, then seemed to give up. "Okay. Just take it easy. Get some sleep. The more you sleep, the quicker you'll heal."

He didn't want to sleep. He wanted to take care of the business he'd come for, but he felt the sting of an injection before he could protest, and then he was sinking into nothingness again.

He clawed his way back up and out of that dark tunnel a few hours later. The apartment was cold and quiet. Shadows seemed to be hemming him in. He stretched and tried to get up, but his muscles weren't working properly. The ache in his leg was dulled but not forgotten.

Painfully, he began to pull himself up. He tried to stand, but he began to cough. Pain shot through his chest and his legs buckled under him. He was going down, turning just in time to make it back into the big, overstuffed chair. He sat there and caught his breath and tried to figure a better way to do this. A way that might work, for instance. But nothing came to mind. There was no one to help him, no one to talk to. It was easier just to go to sleep again.

Kim's shift was almost over and she could hardly wait to get back on that bus. Her eyes were stinging, she was so tired. Lack of sleep tended to do that to her. It had been hard to forget there was a strange man who despised her sleeping just a few feet away. And then Dede had been fussy during the night and had kept her up for hours.

If only she could figure out what was wrong with Dede, why she spent so much time wincing in pain, why her sweet little eyes looked so troubled. Everyone tried to convince her it was just colic, but her instincts told her it was more than that. It just wasn't normal.

She'd given birth to her baby just nine months before in a little seaside town called Dorcher Cliffs. It was a sweet little place, very rustic and charming, and her mother—her real mother!—had bought a local cottage there years ago and left it to Kim when she died. The war had been over for a few months at the time and the sullen men who had survived were still straggling home. It was no fun being on the losing side of a struggle. There was usually a lot of pain and hardship involved.

And one of the worst hardships, right from the beginning, had been the shortage of doctors. Kim had only seen one during all her pregnancy and Dede's birth was attended by a midwife. Luckily, there were no problems and everything went smoothly. But by the time she was six weeks old, Kim knew there was something wrong.

At first she'd bought the line everyone gave her that it was just a normal bout of colic. But she'd known colicky babies and as the months passed, she began to have to face the fact that this was something else—something worse. No one wanted to believe her, but she was Dede's mother and she could tell.

And so began the hunt for a decent pediatrician. There weren't any in Dorcher Cliffs and she couldn't find any in the neighboring towns. So she packed up and they headed for Tantarette. She'd been sure she would find someone easily in the largest city still under Granvilli control. Unfortunately, it hadn't turned out as she'd thought. Everywhere she turned, people were complaining about the lack of medical care available. It was just as bad as it had been in her little village.

Some said the doctors had all been captured by the DeAngelis royals and put in camps and not allowed to go home once the war was over. Others claimed they had mostly defected voluntarily, going for the better pay and more modern facilities the other side controlled. In any case, there were few to be found and pediatricians seemed to be in the shortest supply of all.

So she'd done the only other thing she could think of. She'd taken the first hospital job she could find, hoping it would give her access to someone who could help her. So far, she'd had very little luck. No one could tell her anything about what was wrong with her baby.

She'd taken Dede in to the hospital and begged one general practitioner, an internist, and even a nurse practitioner, to give her a quick look. But every times, she heard the same response.

"No fever? No blood? Sorry, Kim, we just plain don't

have time for normal childhood ailments right now. There are too many people damaged by the war that still need our help. Once we clear the system…"

And she couldn't give anyone any solid evidence of what was wrong. It was just her instincts as a mother that made her sure there was something. Something just wasn't quite right.

It was tough being so all alone—tough and frustrating. There'd been a time when she'd been important to the Granvilli regime—almost part of the Granvilli family itself. There'd been a time when she could have called upon her credentials to get more attention from the power structure. But that time was long gone. She'd been shunned, cast off and turned into a nonperson. Now she was alone and she had to deal with everything on her own.

"You going home?" a red-headed coworker named Ruby asked, frowning at a work schedule on the wall.

She nodded. "Just as soon as I finish with that accident victim in bed fourteen." Her gaze flickered that way. The man's injuries reminded her of Jake's, but much worse. He might lose a leg. That made her wonder if Jake knew how lucky he was to have come away from his own accident so lightly damaged.

"Oh yes, I saw him being stitched up. Pretty ugly." Ruby winced. "Reminded me a little too much of a few months ago when the war was going strong."

"The war." Kim shook her head. "Did that ever really happen? Or was it a dream?"

"I wish." Ruby sighed as she turned away. "I just go one day at a time and hope nothing like that ever happens again."

"Me too."

She looked across the room at the bed she was planning to make her last job of the day, hoping she would be able to finish and get out of the ward before someone found something more to keep her here and away from her baby. Morale was low, help almost nonexistent, and there was more work than there was time to get it done.

But in a few minutes she would leave this place and get back to her baby and...and what? Jake Marallis and his tales of phony royal bloodlines?

It made her angry just thinking about it. Why did Pellea think she would fall for this nonsense? The die had been cast long ago and things were as they were going to be. No fits of remorse from the Queen of Restored Ambria could change what had happened. Once betrayed, always wary. And that was what Kim would always be.

The others who had come looking for her had been easy to dismiss. Jake was another story. He was tough and he was ready to do things the others hadn't been prepared to do. She was scared of him and his crystal-blue eyes. They saw too much and held a grudge. She had to think of an escape plan before he got healthy again.

Walking out of the hospital and making her way to the bus stop, she pulled her coat up against the cold wind. At least it wasn't snowing tonight. But it hardly mattered. She knew what she had to do.

First priority—ditch Jake.

Second—find a doctor who could diagnose Dede.

Third—get herself and her baby back to where they belonged, the little seaside cottage they had been living in since Dede was born, far away from city noise and city cruelty.

Put that way, it seemed simple enough. Now to build up the strength and nerve to implement that plan.

Jake raised his head and listened like a swimmer surfacing for air in a pool of cold, cloudy water. He was going to wake up this time. He was determined. He'd been awake a few times before this afternoon, once to make a shaky trip to the bathroom. He'd almost passed out on the way, but he'd made it. He was getting his strength back, little by little.

There were voices in the hall. He recognized Kim's, and after a moment, decided the other was the de-licensed doctor. He could only make out bits and pieces here and there, but something in their tone told him this wasn't an idle chat.

"Look Kim, there's no guarantee…"

"Just the chance to talk to a real specialist…"

"I can't promise you…'

"…worth its weight in gold for Dede…"

"I'll give you the address when you're ready to go. I can't risk…."

"Are you sure he knows what he's doing?"

"Oh yes. He was the very best in my class at…"

"Why is he hiding?"

"He crossed someone in the Granvilli power structure. There's a price…"

"And he has to leave the country?"

"As a favor to me, he said he'd take a look. But you can't tell anyone…."

Jake frowned as they moved down the hall and the conversation got fuzzier. He didn't much like what he thought he'd heard. He couldn't be sure what exactly was going on, but he knew he didn't like it. Taking a deep breath, he forced himself not to drift back to sleep, hitching up higher in the chair.

And then he waited. It was probably only a minute or two, but it seemed forever and he began to drift off again. But he woke with a start only a short time later when Kim came in with Dede in her arms.

He heard her putting Dede down in her crib and he waited to open his eyes when she came into his field of vision. He heard her approach and he looked up.

The first thing he saw was an angel. The light was behind her and it made her golden hair glow as it flew wildly about her pretty face. Her fur coat added to the illusion, and then she threw it off and revealed her trim figure in its slightly snug nurse's uniform and wiped him out for good. He hadn't known he had this thing for nurses. Who knew?

He closed his eyes again. It was just too much. She was going to burn out his retinas.

"How are you doing?" she asked, bending over him. "I'll bet you're hungry."

He shook his head and risked a quick look at her. "Not really," he said. "But I could use a glass of water."

She got him one and he gulped it down gratefully. It not only quenched his thirst, it cooled him down, and finally he could look at her without making a joke out of himself.

"I've got some news for you," she said, dropping down to sit on the arm of the couch.

He looked up. She was close enough to touch, so he was going to have to keep his response to her reined in. He groaned and half laughed at himself. He could barely move, much less make a play for a beautiful woman. Besides, he despised her. He kept forgetting that.

"What's the news?" he asked.

"Your motorcycle is still there. Still chained to the bus bench. I just saw it."

"You're kidding. I would have thought someone would have stolen it by now."

She nodded. "You know what I think it is? It's so old, so ramshackle, it looks like a piece of urban art sitting there. I'll bet people don't think it really works."

She grinned and he found himself smiling into her eyes. He was just too weak to resist.

"And you know what else?" She produced a cardboard box. "I stopped into the café where we were last night. I figured you didn't have time to pay the bill as you dashed out after me, so I wanted to give them some money for that."

He should have known. She was the type. But that impressed him anyway.

"What a model citizen," he noted, trying to sound cynical and failing.

"Of course." She grinned again. She seemed to be in an awfully good mood. "But here's the point. They were just taking another one of their fabulous apple pies out of the oven. I stood there and watched them and I could hardly stand how beautiful it looked." Her eyes sparkled. "So I bought it." She waved it under his nose. "Can you smell that aroma? We will feast tonight!" She laughed, then sobered a bit as she added, "I invited Dr. Harve to join us for pie later. So we'll save it until then."

It was lucky that she jumped up and headed to the kitchen with her prize at that moment. That gave him time to settle down and blot out how adorable she looked when she was excited. He needed to remember who she was. Leonardo's woman. The mother of Leonardo's child. Of all the women in the world, she was exactly the wrong woman for him to start feeling this way about. He had to cut it out, fast.

He made another trip to the bathroom, feeling a bit more sure of his leg than he had before. He looked into the kitchen on his way back. She was hovering over Dede, who was fussing, and she looked as though a lot of her previous happiness had dimmed quickly.

"Something wrong?" he asked, leaning on the door jamb.

She looked up and shook her head. "No, nothing. Dede's just…" She shook her head again. "Listen, I'm fixing you some soup. It'll be ready in about half an hour."

"Thanks. I mean really, Kim. Thanks a lot."

She flashed him a quick smile but without much warmth. "Don't mention it. I'll bet you need more water."

He nodded, looking toward the sink and wondering how he was going to maneuver getting it.

"No problem. Go sit back down. I'll bring it to you."

He nodded again and did as she suggested. He had a feeling she must have been thinking over their dubious ties just as he had and she realized she was in trouble as long as he was here. She wanted him gone. He didn't blame her. But it wasn't going to happen. Not until she agreed to go with him. In the meantime, he had a serious subject he wanted to talk to her about.

He waited for her to come back out again, and she came soon enough, bringing him another glass of water, and also a pair of sports pants.

"Here," she said. "I picked these up in the hospital supply room. They're stretchy so they should go over your leg better than another pair of jeans would at this point."

He took them and nodded. "You think of everything," he noted.

She hesitated. "I felt bad just taking them," she said. "But we give them away free to patients all the time and if you weren't illegal, you would have been there, so…"

He laughed at her. "You're actually finding a way to justify it to yourself. Kim, I'm sure they've had more work out of you than they've paid for. Stop feeling guilty about everything."

She sighed. He drank down the second glass of water just like he'd done the first and she waited for the glass.

"Listen," he said as soon as he'd swallowed the last drop. "I heard you talking to the doc in the hall."

She took the glass from him but gave him a tart look. "You shouldn't listen in to conversations you're not a party to."

He almost rolled his eyes. "No kidding. Thanks for the etiquette lesson, but I've got bigger fish to fry." He grabbed her hand as she started to turn away, holding her there. "What exactly are you planning to do?"

She stared down at him resentfully. "Nothing. Nothing that is any of your business."

His fingers tightened around her wrist. "Kim…"

But she was already shaking her head. "Forget you heard anything at all. It has nothing to do with you."

She was tugging hard on his hold on her and he knew she was going to slip away any second. To keep his grip, he would have to hurt her and he wasn't going to do that.

"Wait," he said, trying to distract her. He knew the topic of the conversation with the doctor had something to do with the baby, he just wasn't sure what it was. Maybe if he understood a little more about the child, he could figure it out for himself. "Tell me what's wrong with Dede. What are you afraid of?"

Her eyes flashed, gazing into his as though trying to see just how much he'd heard. "Never mind," she said forcefully. "You wouldn't understand."

"Kim, wait," he said again. "You've got to be careful. I don't trust that so-called doctor."

She had her hand back and there was a triumphant glint in her smile. "No problem," she said coolly. "Don't worry about me. I don't trust anyone anymore." Her chin rose. "And I especially don't trust you." She turned with a toss of her head and left the room.

He grimaced, looking after her. He didn't like this. Something bad was coming their way. He could feel it.

CHAPTER FOUR

Kim spent the next half hour tending to Dede, feeding her and playing with her and trying to ignore the man in her living room. If only he hadn't appeared in their lives the day before, everything would be so much easier. Just his being here made things more difficult, and knowing what he wanted her to do made them almost impossible.

But she was riding on a bubble of excitement that she'd had since she came back from work and found Dr. Harve waiting for her down the hall with a golden gift. He'd found her a pediatrician. Finally. She was overjoyed at the news.

She only wished she'd been a bit more careful about keeping Jake from hearing any of it. She had to admit there were a few fishy-seeming details. According to the doctor, this children's physician was an old friend from medical school who had somehow become *persona non grata* with the current Granvilli regime and had to get out of town. He was hiding out at a safe house, about to flee across the border into DeAngelis territory. But Dr. Harve had spoken to him and he'd agreed to see Dede the next day. Kim was so relieved. She had to keep reminding herself that one visit to a pediatrician, even a good one, wouldn't necessarily create a miracle cure for Dede—but it was a start!

She made Jake his bowl of soup and took it out to him. He was dozing, but he didn't seem to be falling into the deep, drugged sleep anymore. That gave her pause. She knew what he wanted to do as soon as he was mobile, and she knew she had to have her child out of here before that time came. She would have to be careful judging when that was.

She cleaned up the dishes and when she came out of the kitchen, found Jake up and leaning over the baby's crib. That gave her a start but she quickly realized he was making baby-talk nonsense noises to her and she was laughing up at him. As she watched, Dede grabbed his nose and let out a yell of happiness.

He laughed, but he pulled away. "Babies are cute and all, but they have no idea of how badly they can hurt a guy with those little fingers," he mentioned wryly, rubbing his nose.

"So you're up," Kim noted, assessing his stability. "How do you feel?"

"Like I'm using someone else's legs and they don't fit very well."

She smiled. It was too bad he was so handsome. It would be easier to stay distant with a less appealing man. And the fact that he seemed to like Dede had not escaped her notice. You couldn't help but like people who liked your kids.

"Come in the kitchen," she said impulsively. "You can sit at the table and I'll make you a cup of hot chocolate."

"With marshmallows?" he asked hopefully.

She laughed. "We'll see if I can dig some up."

She made two cups, found marshmallows, and set

them on the table. Dede had started fussing so she went to get her and returned to the kitchen with her baby in her arms. Dede whipped her head around so that she could give Jake a big grin. Obviously, his appeal hit all ages similarly.

"So tell me, what exactly is wrong with her?" he said, studying her as he sipped his drink.

Kim sat down with Dede on her lap. She was never happier than when she was holding her child. The love she felt tended to overwhelm her at times. It blotted out everything , even the knowledge of who her baby's father was.

"She seems fine to you, right? Perfectly normal? Like any other nine-month-old baby?"

He nodded slowly. "She's adorable."

"Oh. Yes, she is." Kim gave her an extra hug. "But she doesn't feel normal to me. I can tell there's something wrong." Her voice got a little shaky. "And nobody believes me."

His eyes narrowed. "What do you think it is?"

She glanced at him. Did he really care or was he just making conversation?

He wasn't saying what most people said. *You're just a nervous first-time mom. You haven't had enough experience to know what she should be like. All babies cry, all babies act like they're in pain. You get used to it.*

He wasn't saying any of those things. Should she take him as seriously as he seemed to be taking her? She wasn't sure she was ready to trust him that far. Not yet.

"I don't know what it is. That's the whole point. I'm trying desperately to find a doctor who can tell me what it is."

He had a thoughtful look, like a professor noodling with an idea. "What does she do that makes you think there's something wrong?"

She looked at him in surprise. He wasn't just humoring her. He wasn't blowing her off like everyone else did. He actually listened and was reacting to what she'd said. He wanted to know the facts. She didn't really want to talk about this with him, and yet, if he was someone who actually respected her fears and wanted details, how could she refuse?

Still, she had to remember that the man despised her, bottom line. He detested her tie to Leonardo, even though he had no clear idea of how that worked at all. And he was probably going to use any information he gleaned against her in some way. And yet... He was taking her opinion seriously. She threw caution to the wind, took a deep breath, and launched into her fears.

"I just feel like something has never been right internally, from the very first. It's not just stomach aches. It's not just gas. It's not just indigestion."

She held her baby to her face, looking at her closely, and then she kissed her tenderly. Her little expression was always so pleasant, even when she was in pain. What a sweetheart her baby was. Tears filled her eyes but she blinked them away.

"Sometimes, when I feed her, she twists her body as though she's trying to get away from it. She writhes, she cries, she grimaces. Something hurts her. And in a different way than normal. I can just tell." She looked at him, sniffling. "Sometimes she cries, but more often, it's little grunting noises."

"Yes," he said, nodding as he watched the two of them together. "I've heard her do that."

Her eyes widened. "You have?"

"Sure. Last night."

She regarded him as though she'd never really seen him before. He believed her. He'd heard it, too. There was a lump in her throat and for a moment, she couldn't speak. Finally someone admitted it. There was something different about her pain.

Now if she could only convince the pediatrician. She had to be very careful not to rush things, to let him get a feel for Dede and how her rhythms worked. And right now, she had to be very careful not to let Jake know what she was planning to do tomorrow. Once she'd packed up her baby and gone to the doctor, she didn't plan on coming back here at all.

But right now, she had to change the subject. If she went on with this and he kept being so understanding, she would break down and cry right here at the table. Anything would be better than that. She couldn't show that much weakness to the enemy.

And she must make no mistake about it, he was the enemy. She couldn't forget that. Taking a deep breath, she tried to smile.

"So tell me about you," she said, her voice shaky. "How did you get here? Into the country, I mean. From what we've been hearing, the border is tight as a drum these days. They say it's almost impossible to get in or out."

He searched her eyes for a moment, as though wondering why she was changing the subject, but then he shrugged.

"I didn't find it all that hard. I walked across down near where the Brielle River meets the Ellis Canal."

She nodded, feeling more secure as Dede picked up a spoon and banged it on the table. "I know the area," she said as she took away the metal spoon and switched

Dede to a plastic one that wouldn't make such a racket. "We used to have summer picnics there."

"I waited until two on a frosty morning when the guards were dozing. No problem. I wasn't even challenged."

"Lucky you."

"I found my way to a farmhouse, slept in the barn and then bought that wreck of a motorcycle you saw me with last night. I found it in the barn and bought it from the farmer's wife in the morning. She was grateful for the cash and overlooked the trespass."

He hesitated, then went on glumly.

"Everyone over here on the Granvilli side of the island seems to be desperate for money."

She nodded. It was true. "There just isn't any. I haven't been paid at the hospital for over two weeks."

He took another sip of his drink and nodded. "That's the way it is when you lose a war," he said dispassionately. "But the motorcycle was a blessing. It let me make my way a lot faster here to Tantarette. I was lucky enough to find a tiny room in a decrepit house, rented by the day. The landlord was a bit suspicious, but I made up a story about how heroic I'd been in the war, on the Granvilli side, of course, and the man reluctantly let me have a place to sleep. I've been there for a few days now."

"Until last night."

"Until last night." He gave her a long, slow smile that looked almost reluctant. "And I spent most of my time searching for you."

Something about that smile made her pulse race a bit faster. "Until you found me on a bus."

"That was pure serendipity. But I recognized you right away."

His gaze caught hers and held. For some reason she didn't seem to be able to look away.

"Did you study pictures before you left the other side?" she asked, meaning it to be a simple question. So why did it come out sounding breathless?

"Many pictures." His voice was low and gruff. "Videos, too."

"Ah." She licked her lips and tried to stay focused. "So how did you know I would be here in the city?"

His smile was wider now. "I came from the winning side in the war. We have actual reports giving us actual information. And we still have money enough to get things done right."

"Good luck with that," she said, but she didn't sound convincingly cynical. There was a sense of his maleness sweeping over her, making her tingle. She was getting lost in his crystal-blue gaze and she couldn't let that happen.

Time to change the subject again. It took an effort, but she managed.

"And what did you actually do during the war?" she asked brightly.

Though he looked startled at her abrupt turnabout, a flash of humor showed he knew what she was doing. "I worked intelligence, mainly," he said a bit evasively. "But I fought my share of Granvilli soldiers."

"And killed a few?" she asked rather acidly.

He shrugged, eyes darkening. "Not as many as you probably imagine. But I made a few sacrifices in hopes of getting a decent regime back in charge."

"You don't think the Granvillis are decent?"

"Do you?"

She drew in a big breath, not wanting to go down that road. "Well, I spent my time in Dorcher Cliffs. Very quiet, off the beaten path. We didn't have many battles there."

"Sounds like a good place to be. Did you manage to miss most of the war?"

"Pretty much." She frowned, remembering. "We did get some unpleasant residual incidents as the war ended, though. Roving gangs, that sort of thing."

He raised an eyebrow. "What sort of gangs?"

"Mostly looting. The older men still in the village banded together to fight them off. And then, for months, we seemed to be flooded with scam artists looking to make a quick buck off the innocent village people."

He nodded. "That's typical, like vultures swooping in to see what they can glean from the weak and wounded after the fight is over."

"Exactly. They preyed on the old people, confusing them with get-rich-quick schemes, and young mothers of babies whose husbands had been killed, trying to get them to give up their babies with promises of money." She shivered, remembering one slimy example she'd had to deal with herself. "We even had fish rustlers, trying to hijack the catches of some of the older fishermen who they didn't think could defend themselves. But our little town really came together to get rid of the menace."

"Your town sounds great. Why did you leave?"

"To find medical help for Dede."

"Oh. Of course."

Suddenly, he was so tired he could hardly keep his eyes open.

"I think I'd better get back to my chair," he said, rising with difficulty. He started to leave, but he stopped and turned back.

"Listen, Kim," he said, looking less sure of himself

than usual. "I…I just want to tell you how much I appreciate all you've done for me over the last twenty-four hours. Without you, I'd probably be in a homeless shelter right about now."

"You're welcome," she said dismissively. "Now just heal and get out of here."

Her small smile softened her words, but he knew she meant them anyway.

"Okay," he said. "But you're going with me."

She stopped and stared at him, searching for chinks in his armor. "I understand that Pellea wants me back," she said softly. "But tell me this. Do you?"

"Do I what?"

"Really want me to go back to the castle. Something in your eyes tells a different story."

He met her gaze for a long moment, then shrugged. "I'm merely a messenger. I have no opinion."

Her eyes flashed. "Liar."

And his response was a grin.

And then he turned and went on into the living room and sank into his chair. All the time he expected her to say something behind him. But she didn't say a thing, and in just a few minutes, he was too far gone in sleep to hear her anyway.

CHAPTER FIVE

"How are you doing, big guy?" the so-called doctor blustered jovially as he came into the apartment an hour later. "Let's take a look at that leg."

"I'm fine," Jake said, glowering back at him. "I think I can handle this myself from here on out."

"Oh really." Dr. Harve looked a bit taken aback. "Well, I brought over some painkillers and—"

"No thanks," Jake said shortly.

He shrugged, looking puzzled. "It's your choice. But hey, the more you sleep, the faster you heal."

Yeah, he'd heard that one before.

"I'd rather leave the channels open so my body can tell me what's going on," he said. "I wouldn't want to be asleep at the switch."

"I don't know. You may regret this about one o'clock in the morning."

Jake fixed him with a cold stare. "We all have our regrets, don't we?"

Dr. Harve began to look like he wished he hadn't come over. "Uh, well…"

Kim came breezing into the room. "Hi, glad you could make it. I'm just fixing the plates. I'm sure you want ice cream, don't you?"

"Ah." Dr. Harve was on more familiar ground now. "My favorite. Apple pie à la mode."

"Why don't you just sit down and talk to Jake, and I'll bring it all out here."

"Uh." He gave a shifty glance in Jake's direction and turned to follow her into the kitchen. "Why don't I just come along and help you?"

"Well, fine." Kim cast a worried look Jake's way. In a moment they were back, bearing plates piled high with delicious confection and cool, creamy vanilla ice cream.

The doctor sat on the edge of his seat, trying hard not to look at Jake. Kim looked from one to the other of the men. For a few minutes, no one spoke but Jake ate his pie with gusto.

"Wow, that was good," he said, smiling at Kim. "Not quite as good as the one we had the other night, but good enough to give it a run for its money."

The doctor's hands were shaking, making his fork rattle against the porcelain plate. It was obvious nerves were making him even more shaky than usual.

Jake looked at him and decided to quit wasting time.

"Listen, I know what's going on," he said. "You're sending Kim to a discredited pediatrician. Someone in hiding, no less. How much is the guy paying you to send her over?"

The doctor paled and looked at Kim accusingly. "I... this is a private arrangement and you have no—"

"What did he lose his license for? The same thing you did?"

Dr. Harve jumped up and at the same time, Kim said sharply, "Jake! This is none of your business."

"Hey buddy," the doctor chimed in. "I don't know where this animosity comes from, but I don't deserve it. I'm just trying to do Kim a favor here." He glared at her. "She wasn't supposed to tell anyone."

"She didn't. I figured it out for myself."

The doctor looked flustered. "Okay. You're so big on handling everything on your own, handle how mad Kim here is going to be if my friend backs out of the arrangement."

Jake's gaze didn't waver. "That would suit me fine. As it is, if she insists on going, I want her to wait until I can go with her. If your pal is such a damn outlaw, she just might need protection. What do you think?"

The doctor was uncharacteristically at a loss for words. He sputtered for a moment, then turned on his heel and stomped out of the apartment, heading down the hall.

Kim turned on Jake, furious. "If you've wrecked this deal for me, I'll…I'll…" And then she was out the door, too, running after Dr. Harve.

Jake leaned back. "And I guess my work here is done," he murmured to himself cynically.

It didn't bother him to have the doc and Kim mad at him. But it did bother him that the man was ready to exploit a woman who was so desperately trying to find answers. He would do what he could to shield any woman from that. There was nothing special about Kim. Nothing at all.

Kim was so angry at Jake, she couldn't even look at him as she came back into the apartment. She'd caught up with Dr. Harve and pretty much mended fences with him, but she was just furious at Jake for making it necessary. Except for the fact that he was recuperating in her living room, he was nothing to her! He shouldn't even be here. She shouldn't have to know him. Where did he get off meddling with her life?

But ignoring Jake and expecting him to stay in his chair wasn't going to work anymore. As she cleaned up the dishes from the apple pie, he came into the kitchen and picked up a dish towel and began to dry the plates as she set them in the rack.

"I know you hate me right now, but, Kim, this little plan is crazy. Are you really ready to go off and take your baby to some kind of crook?"

She rinsed off her hands and turned to glare at him. "He's a doctor. He's a very fine doctor."

He shook his head in wonder. "The only evidence you have of that is that Dr. Harve told you so, and he's a crook himself."

Her mouth opened in outrage. "Why do you say that? You don't even really know him."

"I can tell." He shrugged. "I've seen his type before. Too shifty. Always looking for a way to make some easy money. He'd sell you out for a bottle of Scotch."

Her eyes flashed. "You don't know that."

She started to turn away but he stopped her with a hand on her arm.

"How much have you paid him for what he's done on me, anyway?" he asked.

She hesitated. A part of her didn't want to tell him. But she was pretty low on cash herself. What was more important, making a point in the argument, or getting her money back? Right now she wasn't sure if either were worth it.

"Enough," she said grudgingly, tugging away from his hold on her arm.

"How much?" He pulled out a wallet and began to count out bills. "Take this."

He held the money out to her. She looked at it and shook her head. "You're my guest," she said, feeling sullen. "I won't take your money."

"Oh for God's sake, Kim. You need the money. I know you do. Here." He put the money on the counter and pushed it toward her. She gave him a poisonous look, then carefully pulled two bills out that came close to what she'd given Dr. Harve. Then she pushed back the others.

"Thank you," she said primly as she turned to go check on Dede.

He watched her go, a smile just barely twisting his wide mouth. Despite everything, he got such a kick out of watching her, especially when she was upset at him. She was so darn cute.

The electricity was out. It was after midnight. Dede had been fussing and Kim had been walking her, but then the lights had flickered out and everything had gone black.

Kim put Dede down in her crib, murmured a few comforting phrases, hoping to quiet her so they wouldn't wake Jake, and then she began feeling her way through the living room to find the box of candles she kept near the front door.

"Ouch!"

She hit her bare foot on the corner of the chair where Jake was sleeping and the next thing she knew, not only did she have a foot that hurt like crazy, she was on her back on the carpeted floor with Jake on top of her.

"What the hell?" he growled, realizing this wasn't what he'd thought it was right away. "Kim, is that you?"

"Get off me, you big oaf," she cried, pushing at him as hard as she could.

"Oh. Sorry. I thought…"

But it didn't matter what he'd thought. He needed to get up off her. But she felt so good. He tried to lift himself, but he couldn't quite make it the first time. He wanted to blame it on his bad leg and generally broken-feeling body, but he knew that was just an excuse. He wanted to feel her wonderful body for another few seconds. He wanted to bury his face in her fragrant hair and cup her breast in his hand and…

"Jake!"

He rolled off her, wincing. His gesture of protective security had come at a cost to his bad leg, but he knew he would get over it. Someday. The sense of the imprint of her body against his would last longer.

"You thought I was a burglar?" she said, sarcasm dripping from her tone. "Thanks a lot, Mr. Hero." She scrambled to her feet, shaken but not hurt. "We don't have that much to steal."

He pulled himself painfully back into his chair and stared into the pitch-black darkness.

"I guess the electricity went out?" he said.

"Bingo."

She felt her way to the door and found the box. Taking out a candle, she struck a match and suddenly there was light again. Not much light, but enough to keep from more mistaken identity problems.

She looked at him in the chair and noticed the hard line around his mouth. She knew that meant he was in pain right now. She hesitated, then said, gruffly, "Sorry I woke you up that way."

He looked up at her. "Sorry I took you down that way." Suddenly, he grinned. "But I've got to say, you're the softest thing I've ever tackled. It was downright delicious."

"Hmmph," she said, turning back to her baby. But secretly, she smiled.

Dede was whimpering and Kim's smile soon faded. The poor little thing was having one of her bad spells. Kim did what she could to try to make her more comfortable, alternating rubbing her little belly and bicycling her feet.

Suddenly, she realized Jake had left his chair and was standing right beside her, looking at the baby as well. Dede was writhing, looking miserable. Kim set her lips. Maybe now he would see why she was so anxious to find a pediatrician for her little girl.

"There are some things I don't understand, Kim," he said quietly.

"Like what?"

He looked at her. "Like why you're living this way. Your opportunities are endless."

She groaned and made a face. "Not that again."

"Okay, let's just ignore the fact that the DeAngelis royals want you back at the castle. Let's pretend they don't even exist. Even without them, you have some pretty impressive connections. Dede's father is the most powerful man on this side of the divide. He's the leader of the Granvilli forces. He was the ruler of all of Ambria itself until a year ago. No one is stronger or more feared." He stared down into her eyes as though searching for answers there. "Surely he can get his own baby a decent pediatrician."

She closed her eyes and turned away. That was exactly the nightmare she faced if she couldn't get help for Dede soon. She would have to go to Leonardo.

She would rather die.

But she still had hope. No matter what Jake said, the pediatrician Dr. Harve had found for her was someone she'd heard of before, someone she was sure could help. After she saw him, if she still wasn't satisfied, she would have to begin considering finding Leonardo and making him face up to his responsibilities. But she would exhaust every other possibility first.

Did that include going back to Pellea after all that had happened between them? Could she really go back and face the woman who used to be like a sister to her—and then betrayed her? Could she really return to the people who had left her behind, forgotten all about her, used her to take the brunt of the anger when everything fell apart? That was something she still hadn't come to terms with.

She flashed a look his way. He was watching her, waiting for an answer, an answer she didn't have to give him.

Suddenly she remembered that he'd mentioned a baby of his own that morning, a baby he no longer had. Did that mean the baby had died? Or been taken from him? Hard to know. It wasn't a question you could easily ask someone. She did know instinctively that he wasn't about to tell her unless he had to.

But if he'd had a baby, had he also had a wife? He hadn't mentioned one, but babies usually came with mothers attached. She wondered what his story was. Too bad she didn't feel free enough to ask him.

Dede had gone to sleep. Picking up the candle, she started into the kitchen. Jake followed her. She knew he was still waiting.

"I told you Leonardo was out of the picture," she told him at last, putting the candle on the kitchen table and sliding down onto the front edge of a chair. "It isn't an issue."

She could see that he didn't believe her, but she

didn't care. It was true. She wished she'd never known Leonardo, and yet, how could she say that when Dede wouldn't exist without him? Her little girl was her whole world now.

Suddenly she had an epiphany. Jake had a thing about Leonardo. He wanted to find him and… Who knew what he wanted to do? But she knew he wasn't planning a friendly chat. He wanted a confrontation of some sort. The animosity he felt fairly bristled off him. That was why he'd come on this mission for Pellea. He was after Leonardo. That was what all the anger was about. Who knew, maybe he even wanted to kill him. Many people had wanted that before.

And he thought he could find the man through her? The funny thing was, she probably detested Leonardo even more than he did.

She didn't know where he was. He certainly wasn't living with her. Not now, not ever.

She looked at Jake speculatively as he sank carefully onto the chair across the table from her. Maybe it would be best to get this out in the open and let him know he was barking up the wrong tree.

"What is the deal with you and Leonardo?" she asked directly. "Why are you so fixated on him?"

Jake looked startled. "I'm not fixated on him. I hate his guts. Other than that…" He shrugged.

"You're not alone," she noted wryly, head to the side as she studied him in the candlelight. The flickering flame made interesting shadows on his skin. What was it about candlelight that seemed to create a circle of intimacy?

He grimaced. "I don't suppose I am. But that's all part of the mystery." Turning his head, he looked into her face again. "What do you find appealing about the man?"

She shook her head. "I'm not going to talk about that," she told him.

"No?" His mouth hardened. "And yet, there's something there. Something has poisoned you against your family. Is your bond with Leonardo so strong you can't even come home to see the people who love you?"

There it was. She could hear it in his voice. That was what he hated about her. Leonardo. What a joke. But she could feel his anger. He hated Leonardo and therefore he hated that she had been with him. She was tainted in his mind, ruined by having Leonardo's child. The funny thing was, she felt a little bit that way herself.

She hadn't always hated the man. By the time she was fifteen, she was working in the castle, and he'd always been there. His father, the general, had been the ruler of Ambria after the coup that had killed the DeAngelis king and queen. At some point Kim's mother, Lady Constance Day, had gone back to work in the castle and she'd gone along. For some reason it seemed to give her mother special cachet in the new regime to have been Queen Elineas DeAngelis's favorite lady-in-waiting, and it was just assumed that Kim would follow in her mother's footsteps. She'd started out as a companion to Pellea and soon became head of social services for the important ladies of the Granvilli regime. She'd been an important member of the household and everyone had seemed to respect and honor her.

Leonardo was older, but she'd found him rather droll and amusing at the time. He'd always wanted Pellea. Pellea's father, a top minister to the Granvilli government, had pushed the match, though Pellea herself resisted.

Then Pellea fell in love with Monte, crown prince of the deposed royal family scheming to make a comeback, and suddenly she was pregnant. Thinking she could never have Monte for her own, she'd agreed, reluctantly, to become engaged to Leonardo. Kim had been there to witness their bond through its many stages.

But when Monte came back to claim Pellea, it was Kim who helped hide him and smoothed the way for the couple to be with each other. Finally, she'd helped her mistress run away to join Crown Prince Monte, and she'd covered it up at the time.

Leonardo was not pleased. She shuddered, remembering.

Then came the war. The DeAngelis royals restored their monarchy and sent Leonardo and the rest of the Granvillis packing, leaving them to cling to the far side of the island with their diminished ranks.

At the time, she'd had no idea the man would end up being so important in her life. He was the most important man in her country—and the father of her child. But he was also a good part of the reason their side had failed in the war. And he'd certainly done what he could to make sure her life would never be the same again.

"I'm not with Leonardo anymore," she said carefully. "I thought I'd made that clear."

His eyebrow quirked as though he didn't believe a word of it.

"When do you see him?"

She stared at him, eyes wide. "What makes you think I ever see him?"

"He's the father of your child."

Pain cut through her like a knife. A lump rose in her

throat for some reason and she coughed, trying to get rid of it before he noticed.

"All this is none of your business," she told him, trying hard to maintain a cool exterior. "Just leave it alone. And believe me, my refusal to go back there has nothing to do with Leonardo."

She bit her lip. Actually, that was a lie. He had a lot to do with it. If it hadn't been for what Leonardo had done…

Oh well. That was not Pellea's fault. Was it?

Was that the choice she faced? If the pediatrician didn't work out tomorrow, she was going to have to choose. Leonardo, or Pellea? One or the other. The devil or the deep blue sea. Only she wished she would never have to see either one of them ever again. Either way, it would be a soul-wrenching experience.

How had everything become so insane? She blamed the war. It made people do things they would never have done otherwise. People died, people had to leave their homes, people found themselves in situations they hated—all because of the war.

"So when am I going to get this special information that is going to change my life?" she asked Jake, thinking of what he'd said when they first met.

"Right now, if you wish," he said. He'd been staring at the table and now he looked up, his blue eyes crinkling. "Ready?"

"Of course."

"All right." He leaned forward, elbows on the table, ready to reveal all to her. "You see…"

"Wait."

Suddenly, she was scared. Her heart was beating like a caged bird in her chest. What if it really did change everything? Was she ready to confront that? Maybe it would be better just to ignore this and let life move on.

"What's the matter?"

She put a hand over her chest. "I can't breathe."

He grabbed her free hand and held it tightly. "Take it easy, Kim. It's good, not bad. I think you'll realize that once you hear what I've got to tell you."

She stared at him with huge eyes but she didn't try to pull her hand away, even though she knew it was trembling in his.

He smiled at her. "Hey, breathe," he ordered.

She took a deep one and nodded. "Okay. Let's have it."

"Here goes." His fingers curled more tightly around her hand. "You know that the Granvilli clan burned the castle and killed Queen Elineas and King Grandor."

She nodded stiffly.

"The royal couple had seven children, five boys and two girls. It was assumed at first that all of them had been killed, but little by little, years later, rumors began to spread that they might still be alive. It turned out that each child had been taken by someone who worked for the royal family and raised as one of their own. Their identities had to be protected to save them from the murderous Granvillis."

She'd been listening passively up to that point, but now she tried to yank her hand out of his. He held on.

"You know they were murderous, Kim. Especially the old general. Facts are facts."

She closed her eyes for a moment, but she didn't say anything.

"You also know that a few years ago, the three old-est boys found each other and began to work on rallying the Ambrians to take their country back. The war came, and they were successful."

She nodded.

"In the meantime, two more of the boys have shown up, so all five have been found."

"What about the girls?" she asked. "Weren't there twin girls?"

"Yes," he said, surprised that she knew that much about them. "No evidence of their whereabouts has ever been found."

"Oh." Her eyes looked very sad for a moment. "How old would they be?"

"I'm not sure. In their late twenties, I'd say."

She nodded, her eyes haunted. She was thinking of how she would feel if Dede were taken from her and she couldn't find her again for twenty-five years. It broke her heart to think of such a thing.

"But now it turns out there was a third girl."

She turned her gaze to him, fear flashing in the depths of her eyes.

He shook his head, wishing he knew how to convince her this wasn't the end of the world. "Queen Elineas had a baby girl born just before the Granvillis struck. No one ever knew, as they kept it secret, fearing what was about to happen to them and their monarchy."

Kim's face was set now. She stared at the wall, no hint of what she was thinking. But something about the tilt of her head reminded him of a painting he'd seen of Anne Boleyn, waiting for the executioner.

"Kim, that beautiful little girl was claimed by one of the queen's favorite maids as her own. She took her home with her when the fighting began. She raised her. And Kim...that little girl was you."

"No," she whispered, still staring at the wall and

slowly shaking her head. "My mother was Lady Constance. She was older when she had me. That's why she didn't tell anyone until it was all over. It was quite a surprise to her that all went so well. But she always told me that having me was the biggest joy of her life." Turning slowly, she stared at him, her eyes dark in the candlelight. "She would have told me the truth," she said softly. "She would have told me before she died."

He shrugged. What could he say to her about that? Anything he thought of sounded like a made-up excuse and he didn't want her to think he was conning her. He was telling her truth and he wasn't going to set up doubts by adding salesmanship.

"I don't believe it," she said firmly, then gazed at him in defiance. "Someone is just tricking you. This is all crazy. I don't want to be a DeAngelis. I don't want to be a stupid princess of the realm. I want to be who I am." Tears welled in her eyes and her voice broke. "I want to be left alone."

She rose clumsily, almost overturning her chair, and went to the sink, turning on the hot water as high as she could and scrubbing the sink with a brush.

"Kim." He rose and stood close to her, wishing he knew what to say. Tentatively, he reached out and touched her hair. "Why don't you give it some time. Why don't you…"

She turned to face him, her eyes shooting daggers through the tears. "Why do you expect me to accept all this from you? You hate me."

He was taken aback. "Hate you? Why would I hate you?"

"Admit it. I can see it in your eyes. Every time you mention Leonardo."

"Hey." He took her by the shoulders, looking down into her face. "I'll admit to hating *him*. But you..."

"You despise me because I slept with him." Her chin rose in a teary challenge. "Don't you?"

He hesitated. He wasn't even sure that was true any longer. But his hesitation made her more sure of it.

"See? You can't deny it."

"Yes, I do deny it," he protested. "I may have felt that way at first."

"Yes, you made it very plain. I'm not much good." She turned away, her shoulders shaking and her voice breaking. "Me and my...my...Granvilli baby."

A sob broke through her misery and he couldn't take it any longer.

"Kim." He pulled her into his arms and up against his chest, gasping as she hit the ribs, but not about to stop her for it. "Kim, don't. You have nothing to cry about. Really."

He looked down and she looked up, her face wet and beautiful, and he bent down and kissed her. He hadn't planned that. If he'd thought things through, he never would have done it. But the moment came and he kissed her.

"Oh!"

She was surprised, but she didn't pull away. He was big and he was male and he smelled so good. His kiss was perfect, gentle and comforting rather than aggressive. There was no demand in his touch, no urgency, but the sensuality was an extra thrill, a sweet and sexy charge of electricity that couldn't be ignored.

It had been so long since she'd felt the protective arms of a man around her. She couldn't help but let herself sink into it. It was so extraordinary, so wonderful.

"Even better than a hot shower," she whispered to

herself as he began to draw back. Her eyes were still closed. She was savoring the moment.

"What?" he said, frowning at her and wondering what he was getting himself into at the same time. He shouldn't have kissed her. But he couldn't really say he regretted it. She tasted as good as she looked—sort of sweet and tangy, like a lusciously ripe citrus fruit. It was a taste he was pretty sure would linger with him.

"You feel good," she told him, blinking rapidly and backing away. "But I still don't want to be a princess. And I still think you hold Leonardo against me. And Dede."

He shook his head, taking her seriously. It was true that the thought of her being with Leonardo made him cringe inside. The man was such scum, he couldn't understand why any woman would let him anywhere within touching distance. Still, that didn't mean the baby was to blame.

"No one can ever fault the baby," he said reasonably. "They have no say in the matter."

She looked up at him, her eyes dry now, but filled with a rueful sense of irony. "And you think *I* did?"

His head jerked in her direction. "What do you mean by that?"

She turned her head away. "Nothing. Nothing at all."

"Kim…" There was something there, but he lost it when she turned back and touched his cheek with the palm of her hand, making his heart jump in his chest.

"Take care, Jake. Be good to your sister. She needs a champion like you to guard her. Things are likely to get a lot rougher before we heal this rift."

He grabbed her hand and wouldn't let her withdraw it. "What are you talking about?" he asked her. "You sound like you're saying goodbye."

"Do I?" She shook her head and gave him a sad smile. Her gaze ranged restlessly over his handsome face. "I'm just so tired, I don't know what I'm saying. I'm going to bed."

She pulled on her hand and he let it go reluctantly.

"When is your appointment tomorrow?" he asked before she had a chance to leave the room.

She looked back at him. Her eyes were hooded. "In the afternoon. Two o'clock."

His mouth hardened. "Where is it?"

She shrugged. "I don't even know yet. Dr. Harve said he'd tell me just as I left, so as not to risk anyone else knowing."

He grunted, annoyed. "Me, he meant."

Her sad smile was back. "Maybe."

He looked at her assessingly. "Are you going into work in the morning?"

"No. I'm staying here. I took the day off."

He nodded. "All right, then." He watched as she started out of the kitchen, into the gloom, and he went to the doorway and called her back one last time.

"Kim, don't go to the man," he said, the urgency of his feelings clear in his voice. "It's no good and you know it."

She shook her head, but before she could speak, he went two steps closer and took both her hands in his, gazing at her earnestly.

"There's a simple solution to all this, of course. And you know what it is."

"No." She shook her head so hard her hair whipped across her face.

He held her hands tightly. "Go back with me to the castle and you'll have access to all the medical help and the best facilities you could ask for." He almost wanted to beg her. "It's a short trip across the island, Kim. I can take you there in one day."

She gave him another sample of her sad smile and slipped her hands out of his, then headed for her bedroom.

"We'll talk more in the morning," he said hopefully.

She nodded, looking back at him, and this time she made it to her room.

She'd lied about the time of her appointment. It was ten in the morning. She planned to get out of here with her baby, go to the appointment, and not come back to the apartment. That would mean finding another place to stay for a week or so. By then, hopefully, Jake would give up and go back to the castle without her.

Could she get away with it? Why not? If the pediatrician turned out to be as good as they said he was, it was worth a try. Only time would tell how this would all shake out.

One thing was sure—she wasn't going to be a DeAngelis princess. And she wasn't going back to be Pellea's pet again. Not ever.

CHAPTER SIX

THE morning sun scattered her fears and doubts like blossoms in a strong spring breeze. What had she been thinking last night? She'd let a combination of the electricity failing, being awake after midnight, the crush of all her troubles, and finally, Jake's influence, put her in a very bad place—a place where she didn't have to be. So when he'd come at her with this crazy story about her being royal, and tried to convince her it was serious, she'd been very low on defensive power and couldn't resist the emotions he'd conjured up for her.

This whole fantasy that the royals were trying to foist on her was complete nonsense. She'd heard bits and pieces of it before and had dismissed it out of hand. She knew who her mother was, she knew who had raised her and loved her and made her into the person she was today. For them to try to tear apart her reality and destroy the feelings she had for the only person in this world who ever truly loved her, just to force her to come back to their side, was despicable as far as she was concerned. She wasn't going to let them.

As for Jake—she couldn't believe he could actually be in on it, not fully. She was pretty sure he thought he was telling her the truth. He just couldn't be that good a liar. Much as they were at dagger's point with each other on a lot of things, she would like to think he at least had the integrity not to fall in with that sort of scheme. Somehow, they had convinced him.

But none of this mattered anymore. After today, she hoped never to see Jake again. And then, hopefully, the messengers from the castle would stop.

They'd been coming for the past six months, one after another. The first had been a young footman named Billy she'd known in the old days. He'd come to her cottage in Dorcher Cliffs with a simple message. Pellea wanted her best friend back and was ready to coax her. What would it take to get her to return?

That one had been easy to laugh off. She'd always liked Billy. That was surely why they had chosen him. So she'd fed him a nice dinner and gave him too much wine so that he'd told her everything—how Pellea and the rest of them were always plotting and trying to arrange matters. As if they didn't have anything better to do. Once she'd found out everything she wanted to know, she'd sent him packing.

The next came a month later, a nice young girl name Posey who had a flair for the dramatic. Kim had known her mother when she worked in the castle kitchen in the past. Posey pretended to know dangerous secrets and hinted around about dark spells and magic potions and foundlings who had to be returned to their proper places. Kim couldn't make heads nor tails of what she said, but when she announced that saying any more would endanger them both and might send Kim to the royal dungeon, she'd had enough and sent her packing as well.

And they were only the first two. Others came over the border to find her. None was very effectual. They begged, they pleaded, they claimed that Pellea was moping about for want of her best friend. Kim didn't believe a word of it and she stopped even being polite about it.

But Jake was the first to find her since she came to the city. He was also the one with most stature and rank, making her wonder why Pellea would send such an important person. But then he began trying to peddle a story of misplaced birth mothers even more seriously than the others. Hah. She didn't believe a word of that, either.

She was picking up clutter in the living room when Jake opened his eyes. He looked at her. She looked at him. The memory of what had happened the night before grew between them and before she knew it, they were both laughing.

"You know that it all didn't mean a thing, don't you?" she insisted right away. "You realize it was all part of the usual night terrors you get when the shadows are too thick and the time is too late."

He growled at her. "Are you saying that kissing me reminds you of your most ugly nightmares?" he asked softly.

"No, of course not." She laughed again, shaking her head. What was she saying, anyway? She wasn't sure. Luckily, Dede was crying and she had an excuse to turn away from him.

Dede wasn't doing very well this morning. Her little lower lip was pouted out and Kim could see the pain in her. Still, her pretty little eyes tried to smile. She was the sweetest of babies. Kim's heart broke, watching how hard she tried to remain cheerful, and something fierce grew inside her. She would do anything for this baby. No one was going to stop her from taking her to the pediatrician. Nobody.

"Have you been listening to the news?" Jake asked a

bit later, after Dede had been calmed and fed and was cooing happily in her crib.

There was no television in this skimpily furnished apartment, but Jake had found an old radio and listened to it now and then.

"No," she said, surprised by his tone. "What's going on?"

"It looks like the Granvilli government—or what's left of it, is about to fall apart. They say the only thing that could save it would be for Leonardo to show up and rally the factions to work together again. But nobody seems to know where he is." Staring at her, he raised one dark eyebrow.

She blinked. "Don't look at me. I've told you over and over again that he has nothing to do with my current life."

He nodded, noting the careful way she'd put that. On one level, he believed her. Why? Just basically because she was the sort of woman who tended to tell the truth. But there was so much more going on than simple relationships could encompass. There were international ties and incidents and remnants of war and power struggles. As someone had said once, their lives didn't matter a hill of beans compared to the major forces gathering and preparing to vie for power, wealth and influence. The big boys were at their games, and the regular people had better get out of the way if they could. They were the ones who tended to get hurt when the last card was played.

"You do realize that this isn't going to last," he told her calmly. "They might pull the government together one more time, Leonardo might even show up and rekindle some spirit, but it's all just in one big holding pattern. Everybody's waiting for the end."

"I'm not," she said stoutly, casually folding some baby clothes to put into the bag she was going to take with her and hoping he wouldn't think a thing of it. "For me, the end came long ago. I'm busy dealing with the fallout."

He frowned, not sure what she could mean by that. But he let it go. He was tired of arguing. What would be, would be.

"The whole of society is falling apart," he told her rather dolefully. "You can't find a decent doctor. The police are nowhere to be seen. Electricity is unreliable, cell phone service is out. I wonder how Wifi is doing. The country is regressing to conditions of a hundred years ago."

She kicked a baby blanket out of her path, annoyed with him for going on this way. Deep in her heart, she knew it was probably true. But what good did it do thinking about it now? There was nothing she could do about it. Besides, her goals were more short-term at the moment.

"The DeAngelis royals are eventually going to come in and take over this side of the island, too," he said flatly, following her progress through the room with his crystal-blue gaze. "You know it. And what are you going to do then?"

"I'll deal with that when it happens." She threw him a quick glare. "Maybe I'll just go further into the mountains. There are people up there who have lived away from the rest of Ambrian society for decades, you know."

"Okay. I see. You'll join the mountain people." He grinned, obviously amused. "Hey, that sounds like fun. Maybe I'll come with you."

She resisted the temptation to grin back at him. He would be fun if she would only let him be. She knew that. But she also knew that it didn't pay to get too friendly with people. You began to rely on them, and then they always let you down. And sometimes, they did worse than that.

She glanced at the clock. The minutes ticked by. In another hour, she would be arriving at the pediatrician's location. She only hoped and prayed that he would be able to help Dede.

She'd packed away her baby's things and a bottle in case she needed it. She was pretty much ready to go. The only thing that was worrying her now was whether or not Jake would go back to sleep before the time came for her to grab Dede and go.

To her chagrin, she'd actually played around with the idea of trying to drug him. She certainly had enough medicine still hanging around from what Dr. Harve had given him that first day. But when it came right down to it, she couldn't do it. It just wasn't right. If he didn't go to sleep, she would tell him she was taking Dede to the park and she would slip out anyway.

And then—a miracle. She looked over at him, and Jake was asleep in the big, deep chair. Her heart jumped and she went quickly to her notebook, tore a paper out and wrote him a quick message. Then she gathered together as many of Dede's things as she could possibly carry and gave one last glance at Jake. It gave her a pang to see him sleeping there, oblivious to what she was doing. He was so handsome. She looked at his full, beautiful lips and smiled as she remembered the kiss. She paused a second longer, itching to reach out and brush back the dark hair that had fallen over his forehead. But she couldn't risk waking him.

It was time to go.

* * *

Jake woke up almost an hour later. He stretched, yawned and glanced around. There was no one in sight. Suddenly, the eerie quiet of the apartment was ominous. It didn't sound as though someone had left the apartment and would be back soon. It sounded as though someone had left and was never, ever coming back. How he could tell the difference, he wasn't sure. But he knew it.

Rising from the chair, he hobbled to the bathroom, then did a quick tour of the room. Kim had taken the big bag she used to carry Dede's things in. That didn't necessarily mean anything. She took it everywhere. But something didn't feel right.

And then he saw the note. He went quickly to the table and dropped into a chair before he picked it up.

Dear Jake,
I think it's only fair if I let you know, I'm taking Dede to the pediatrician. We're going earlier than I told you. Sorry that I felt I had to lie to you. I won't be coming back. You won't be able to find me again, so you might as well go back and give Pellea my regrets. Once again, I must refuse her generous offer.
    Goodbye, Jake. Take care.

Crumpling the paper in his fist, he growled his anger. Rising slowly, he tested his leg. It was still painful, but that was just too bad. He wasn't going to let it hold him back. Not this time.

Then he hesitated. He couldn't go anywhere with his jeans pants cut almost to the crotch. His gaze fell on the pants Kim had snagged for him at the hospital. Quickly, he tugged off his jeans and put on the stretchy pants. They weren't stylish, but they would do the job. He grabbed his coat and slammed out of the apartment, heading for Dr. Harve's place.

He found it at the second door he tried. Dr. Harve opened the door and immediately looked as though he regretted it.

"Oh. Hello. I was just…"

Jake didn't wait for niceties. He used his forearm as a bar at the doctor's throat and pushed him back against the wall.

"Give me the address," he demanded coldly.

The doctor sputtered, choking. "I…I don't know what you're talking about."

He jammed his arm at the throat harder, in no mood for mercy. "You know she's in danger. Give it to me."

The doctor turned bright red, choking and gasping for air. "No, no, I gave her the name of a friend of mine. He's a fine doctor, really…." He was now almost turning blue.

Jake relented long enough to let him get a breath. "Good men can turn bad when they get desperate," he pointed out harshly. "And from what you've said about this guy, he's desperate."

"Oh no." He grabbed at his bruised neck, his voice sounding as if it was coming from the bottom of a food mill. "Not Henry."

"Give me the address. Now."

His eyes flared and he tried to pull away, looking frightened. "I can't give it to you, I promised."

Jake's hand grabbed his throat and he picked him up by it, smashing him against the wall behind him.

"Give me the address, you bastard," he snarled. "You just sent Kim and her baby into a trap and you probably suspect it yourself."

"No, no! You've got it all wrong."

He pushed him back harder. "Give it to me now or I'll break your damn neck."

Dr. Harve made a strangling sound, flailing like a rag doll, but Jake could make out parts of a word that sounded like acquiescence. He let him drop, but stood close enough to threaten him, and Dr. Harve reached into his jacket and produced a crumpled paper.

"Here," he said, his voice sounding ruined. "Now get out of here. I've got a gun, you know."

"Really?" Jake took the address and put it into his pocket, then looked down at the man with contempt. "I wouldn't bring it out if I were you. I'd probably just use it to kill you."

And without another word, he was gone.

He had no idea where the address was. His leg ached, but he didn't care. He was driven by time, and he was afraid it might already be too late.

The street outside was empty, and when he got to the main street, a block away, it wasn't busy. Still, there were a few pedestrians who looked like they might know a thing or two. He only had to ask three before he found someone who could tell him where the address would lead him. It was only about a mile away.

"Not a good part of town, however," the man who was helping him warned. "You'd better watch your back in that neighborhood."

"Don't worry," Jake said through gritted teeth. "I'm ready for that."

To his amazement the motorbike was still chained to the bus bench, just as Kim had said it was. He'd have thought someone would have sawed off the chain by now. Maybe that was the advantage of having a bike so old and disreputable that no one else wanted it. He found the key in his coat pocket, and in minutes he was on his way. He had no idea how long ago Kim had left the apartment, but he was pretty sure she either had to walk, carrying Dede, or take the bus. Either way, he was just hoping there was a chance to catch up since he had the advantage with the bike.

Until it ran out of gas.

At first he just stared at it, unable to believe the timing. He had to restrain himself from giving it a kick. But there was no other option than wheeling it along the road until he found somewhere with gas for sale. And he knew from experience that wouldn't be easy.

He kept up a steady chain of swear words under his breath as he walked, angry at himself, angry at fate, angry at Kim, angry at the whole medical profession. And at the same time, he pushed himself to walk as fast as he could on his bum leg. The pain was stabbing now, every time he took a step. It was just this side of impossible to stand, but he felt the urgency of time passing drumming at his back and he had to hurry. He had to get there before…

He tried to tell himself that he didn't know for certain that the man was a crook and a kidnapper. But he was pretty sure that was the case. If Kim lost Dede just because he ran out of gas, he wasn't sure he would be able to live with himself.

Another thing bothered him. He was regretting that he'd left Dr. Harve in one piece. What if he found a way to call his friend and warn him? That would not be good. He had to go faster. If only the stupid bike hadn't crapped out on him.

And then—a miracle! A gas station that actually had some gas. He wheeled his bike up to the pump and filled the tank. New life—for him and his motorcycle.

Another moment and they were off through the winding streets.

"Hold on, Kim," he muttered into the wind. "Just hold on a few minutes longer."

It took much too long to find the address. He went up and down streets, asking everyone he could find. But as his original helper had said, it was a bad neighborhood. People weren't very forthcoming in a place that smelled like too many people used the sides of buildings as a lavatory.

He retraced his steps, knowing it had to be there somewhere but unable to pin it down, and panic started to claw at his gut.

"I'm coming, Kim," he muttered, almost in despair. "If I could just find the damn…"

And suddenly, there it was, the street sign hidden behind a large parked truck. He turned and found the building right away, stashing the bike and taking the crumbling stairs two at a time, biting back the cry of pain that tried to come up his throat. He found the number and he didn't bother to knock, thrusting the door open and staring into Kim's wide eyes.

"You're still here," he panted out, struggling for breath. "Thank God."

She was furious, her face strained, her eyes huge with anger.

"What are you doing here?" she demanded. "How dare you interfere with my life this way? How did you find me, anyway? Did you hurt the doctor?"

But he didn't answer any of that. Looking around, he realized she didn't have her baby.

"Where's Dede?" he demanded hoarsely.

"Jake, you can't…"

He grabbed her by the shoulders. "Where the hell is Dede?" he yelled.

She looked at him blankly. "The doctor took her into the examining room, just to weigh her, while I fill out these papers. They should be back any second."

Something about Jake's tone and the look in his face was finally communicating the seriousness of the situation to her. She still didn't believe anything was wrong. But if Jake was this worked up, maybe she ought to check.

Jake couldn't wait for her to decide what was important and what wasn't. He pushed past her into the area she'd called the examining room. It was empty. He flew to the window and just caught sight of someone disappearing down the outside fire escape.

Kim was screaming behind him but he couldn't stop. He tore out of the doorway and down the metal stairs, jumping the last portion. He'd never run so hard before in his life. His entire being, every part of him, was focused and determined. He was going to get Dede back.

And then he fell, tripping over a cement boundary in a parking lot and coming down hard. He cried out in pain, but a part of his consciousness wouldn't accept it. He had no time for pain. Leaping back to his feet, he ran again, more determined than ever.

He saw a long black car ahead, a driver waiting, and he knew that was the destination. He could see the snatcher, judge their relative distances from the car, and he knew he would never catch him in time. He had to think fast. Another few seconds and it would be too late. Dede would be gone forever.

They would never find any police who would help them in time. The snatcher would have her out of the country before they even found someone who would take a report.

He knew he would never catch the snatcher by following behind. He had to take a chance. Instead of running down the sidewalk behind him, he took a short cut, leaping on the back of a parked car, and from there, onto one that was moving.

The people inside began to yell and the driver looked for a place to pull over, but he got a good start and when he leaped from the stopping car onto another that was moving in the right direction, he got another boost.

He was gaining, but not enough. He could see the so-called pediatrician about to jump into the long black car. Everything in him made a surge. He almost thought he could fly, if he just willed it. And this time he took a wild, insane short cut across three cars, and from there he dove, tackling the snatcher around the legs just before he stepped into the car.

He felt bones crunch and heard the yell of injury from the snatcher, but his focus was all on Dede, and he saw the man let her go as he fell. She was wrapped in a blanket, but she landed hard on the cement. Jake aimed for her, leaving the man behind as he sailed across the space between them and grabbed her. She was crying, hiccupping in hysterics, and he held her close, then turned to see the snatcher disappear into the car and the car take off like a bat out of hell.

He suddenly realized that he hadn't been breathing enough. His chest felt as though it had caved in. He gasped for air and the pain from his cracked ribs was excruciating. But he held Dede, cooing sweet comfort into her tiny baby ear, and thanking every spirit and god he could think of for the victory.

Suddenly, Kim was there. She didn't say a word, just

opened her arms for her baby, and he handed her over. There was a bump growing on Dede's forehead and a bloody scrape right beside it, but she stopped crying once her mother was holding her.

And Jake collapsed in a heap on the sidewalk.

"Crazy insane. Both of us were crazy insane. Me, for trying to convince myself it would be okay to go to that awful man. And you for saving Dede the way you did."

She shook her head, staring at him in wonder again as she had been for the past half hour.

"You flew. I saw you. You were in the air, flying, as though just the force of your will could make it happen." She threw up her hands, shaking her head. "It was like in a movie. If I hadn't seen it myself, I wouldn't believe it."

Jake didn't say anything. His head was back and his eyes were closed. They were in a small coffee shop, sitting in a corner booth, drinking iced tea and trying to recover from what had just happened.

"By all rights, I should have broken my neck," he said, pretty much in awe of it all himself. "Or at least my leg. My bad leg. The one I can hardly walk on. But somehow, it all worked."

"Adrenaline," Kim said, nodding. "That is what it had to be."

"Maybe. Or just a little magic." He straightened and looked at her, then looked down at a sleeping Dede in her arms. A feeling of overwhelming happiness washed over him and he frowned, forcing it back.

Okay, so he saved this woman and her baby. He was lucky. And no, it didn't make up for not saving his own wife and his own baby that awful day. Nothing could make up for that.

But it was still good. So good. He took a deep breath and then he sighed. Okay. He was going to allow himself a little happiness. Hey, he deserved it. Didn't he?

"How did you know?" she asked him, dropping a kiss on Dede's downy head. "How did you know he would turn out to be a crook?"

"I didn't know for sure. But the signs were all bad." He shook his head. "This is what it's often like when you lose a war. It brings the best out in some people, but too many lose sight of their humanity and resort to any means to survive." He glanced at her sideways. "And those roving bands of child snatchers you said appeared in Dorcher Cliffs a few months ago have shown up all over the island. It's just that on the Granvilli side, law and order is breaking down. You see it everywhere."

She nodded. She knew it was true.

"You know there are plenty of people on the continent who want babies and can't have them for one reason or another. A lot of them will pay plenty for a child they can adopt. And many don't care where they came from."

She sighed. "I know that. It's just hard to believe when it comes this close to you." She shook her head. "To think of Dede in that man's control." Her voice broke and she looked down at her child. The lump was going down and she'd cleaned up the scrape with water in the bathroom. But it could have been so much worse. She shuddered.

Jake was thinking about the same thing, just thankful that he'd taken out after her when he did. If he'd slept another half hour…

He glanced up at Kim. She was looking thoughtful and his antennae went up.

"What now?" he said softly. "What's the plan?"

She looked at him, her dark eyes candid. "I want to go home," she said.

"To the castle?"

"No!" She glared at him. "That's not home. Dorcher Cliffs is home. I told you, I have a cottage there. I was raised in it until...until I went to the castle."

He nodded slowly. "Great," he said. "Let's go."

She started to laugh. "I don't remember inviting you to come along," she noted.

"That's where you're wrong. There was the distinct element of invitation in your voice. I heard it loud and clear."

"Really?"

"Yes, really." He reached out and grabbed her hand in his. His eyes were dark and serious as he gazed into hers. "Do you think I'm going to let you go anywhere by yourself after what happened today?"

She was shaking her head, but she was still laughing.

But he wasn't amused. "You've got to stop running from me," he said. "I'm not the enemy, Kim."

"Okay." She sobered. "I won't run away from you. But..."

"I know." He nodded. "You don't want me to think you've given in. I understand. That doesn't mean I'm going to quit working on it." He flashed her a quick smile. "But I don't expect you to cave in. Not yet."

She sighed. She knew she was supposed to be guarding herself against him, but after what he'd done now, how could she hold him off the way she had before? Impossible. She leaned toward him.

"We're partners now, right? I need to go where I can think about things. I'm going to decide what's best for me to do. But I've got to get some stability, some peace and quiet. I need to go to the cottage."

"I agree. I think it would be good for you—and for Dede."

"Yes. We can stay there. We can talk things over and…we'll see." She gave him a warning look. "But I want your word that you won't pressure me. You're not going to try to grab me and throw me over your shoulder and drag me to the castle, are you?"

"Mixed metaphor, kind of," he noted. "I can't drag you if you're on my shoulder."

She punched his arm. "You know what I mean. Are you?"

"I swear to you I won't do that."

The waitress brought the sandwiches they'd ordered. Jake ate his ravenously, but Kim couldn't eat. She was still in shock, at least emotionally, over what had happened.

What if Jake hadn't arrived when he did? What might have happened? It made her hold her baby closer and whisper a little prayer of gratitude.

She glanced around the shabby little café. Someone had strung multicolored lights around the edge of the counter and there was a small Santa Claus by the cash register. At least someone had remembered what the season was. She shivered and looked down at Dede. She wanted an old-fashioned Christmas for her, with snow and Yule logs and horses pulling sleighs.

The trouble was, you didn't get those where they were going. For that, they would have to stay up here in the mountains. She'd never had a Christmas like that herself. So where did she get the sense that it was the ideal? She sighed. Somehow she would make her baby's Christmas special. She would find a way.

"Do you want to go back to your apartment before we head out?" Jake asked her.

She smiled. She thought it was interesting how completely he was invested in this trip already. "No," she said. "I didn't leave much behind and I'm fully paid up for the month." She stopped, suddenly anxious. "What did you do to Dr. Harve?" she asked as she realized he must have done something to get the address of where she was going. "Do you think we should go back and check on him?"

Jake barely met her gaze before his skittered off again. "No," he said shortly. "I'm sure he's okay."

"Uh-huh." She shook her head, but she really didn't want to know the details. "And how about you? Are you okay? You put that body through a lot today. Maybe you should have a day of rest before trying to travel."

"Don't be ridiculous," he scoffed. "I'm ready to go when you are. We can be in Dorcher Cliffs by dinner time."

"Really?" She wrinkled her nose. "How are we planning to do this?"

He looked astonished that she didn't understand that already. "On the motorcycle of course."

"Oh?" Her eyebrows rose. "That sounds exciting. Do we each get our own motorcycle?"

He frowned as though he thought she was being silly on purpose. "No. You'll be riding behind me, holding on for dear life."

She was beginning to realize he really meant it and her eyes got very wide. "On that crummy little thing?" she said, looking out to where he'd locked it to a lamppost.

"Sure. It can handle the load. I'll be careful."

She opened her mouth, but nothing came out. She was speechless.

"It's a fine little machine," he said quickly, reassuring her. "It'll get us there, don't worry."

She stared at him, trying to picture what they would look like flying down the highway. "But…but how will I carry Dede and hold on at the same time?"

"No problem. We'll tie you on. And put Dede in that sling carrier you have and strap her to you. It'll be fine."

"Tie me on?"

"Sure. It's the only way that will work. No one will pay any attention to us. We'll be instantly incognito."

She let out a sigh that was more exasperation than anything else. "Because only fools would ride that way?"

He grinned as though he thought she finally got it. "Something like that."

"Wonderful." Her sarcasm was showing, just a little bit.

He frowned, realizing she really wasn't with the program just yet. "Do you have a better idea?"

She shrugged, wishing she could think of something, fast. "We could take the bus. That's how we got here about six weeks ago. The bus is pretty incognito, too."

His scowl showed her what he thought of that idea. "Not incognito enough. We need to fly under the radar."

She shook her head, at a loss. "Why?"

He hesitated, realizing that was a pretty good question. "Because I'm illegal and you're a runaway princess. Don't you think those are a couple of pretty good reasons?"

Shaking her head, she gave in. Despite all he'd been through, he was the one with more energy, more spunk left. She just felt wrung out and lifeless. She needed to get where she could relax again, something she hadn't done in weeks.

And so she gave him the answer he was waiting for. "All right. I'm ready. What do I do?"

CHAPTER SEVEN

THE snow began as they were leaving the city.

"Don't worry," Kim told Jake. "It never snows in Dorcher Cliffs, or anywhere down near the shore. We'll be out of this soon."

Famous last words.

The bike was steady, but not very fast. As they chugged along, it began to snow even harder. Jake was right about one thing—they were incognito—hidden by the driving snow. There wasn't anyone else on the road to see them, anyway. Most people wisely stayed indoors.

Kim wasn't sure she would make it. Every mile seemed more and more excruciating. The wind whipped her face, snow matted in her hair, her ears were frozen. She had to hold Dede so tightly, she kept wondering if she was about to smother her in all the cloth and binding. What on earth had she let herself in for? This was pure misery. They had to go back.

She let Jake know how she felt when they came to a pause at a crossroads. At first he tried words of encouragement.

"Just think of pioneer women in the American West," he told her cheerfully. "Crossing the snow-covered Sierras in little rickety wagons."

"At least they had some protection from the elements," she noted rather sharply.

"Not a whole lot. Besides, this is only going to last for a few hours, not days or weeks like their journey did."

It was obvious he was having the time of his life. He seemed to thrive in the freezing cold wind. Snowflakes stuck to his eyelashes, making him look even more rakish than usual, and his eyes were shining with adventure. But once he'd looked back into her face, he seemed to realize her complaint was no passing fancy.

He pulled over as they came up to a small shed ahead, pulling out of the weather as much as he could and turning to look at her again.

"If you're really this miserable, we'd better do something about it," he said soberly.

She looked up at him in surprise. Something about his willingness to see her side of things made her feel much better.

"We could find a farmhouse," he suggested. "There have to be a few near here. And maybe they would let us in for a bit. Once the snow lets up, we could go on, or turn back, whichever seems best at the time."

She studied his serious face, wondering how she could ever have thought he looked like a man filled with hate. He seemed to be ready to accommodate her in any way she needed.

"No, you know what?" she said, shocking even herself. "I can do this. I'm just letting myself sink into whining a bit. I'm over it now." After all, the main thing was to get home so she could think things through and decide what she was going to do about finding a doctor for Dede.

He frowned, searching her eyes. "Are you sure?"

"As long as Dede's okay, I can do this."

He glanced down at the baby and smiled. "Okay. Let me know if it gets to be too much." He looked at her speculatively. "We might find an inn, you know. If we do, we'll stop."

She shook her head. "The only inn I know of along this road gets a little wild at night. Let's just push on through. We wouldn't want to stop there."

Wrong again. The one thing she didn't anticipate was that Dede would be so hungry after the crazy day she'd had that she would let fussing turn into outright crying. That was unusual for her. So was the wrestling match she was trying to have with the sling and everything else that got in her way. Then Kim remembered that she'd only fed her once since lunch. In time, the struggle was just too much and Kim had to ask Jake to stop again.

"We're going to have to pull over," she called out to Jake.

"Look," he said. "The inn is just ahead. Why don't we go in there and get warm for a bit before we go on?"

Despite her reservations about the place, the prospect of getting warm sounded like heaven.

"We'll just go in and get a little cup of soup to warm us up and we'll be on our way again," Jake suggested. "Meanwhile you can get that little fussbudget fed."

Once inside, Kim's spirits started to rise. Waves of warmth enveloped them, and then the happy sounds of patrons singing songs and engaging in some good-natured teasing that included a lot of laughter. It seemed a crowded, cheerful scene. A lot of the men looked like they'd only been out of the army for a short time, and some still wore their uniforms—Granvilli green was everywhere.

Once inside the pub, they found a table in the far corner and Jake left them to go to the bar and order a couple of cups of chowder. He was back with the soup moments later, sliding into his seat, turning his face away from the crowd and pulling up his hood over his head.

"Wouldn't you know it?" he said to her. "The one place I see someone I know from the other side and it has to be here and now."

"What?" she asked, alarmed.

His face was grim. "There's someone here who knows me."

She drew in a sharp breath. "Where?"

"See that bunch by the fireplace? The tall fellow with the purple scarf?"

She looked where he'd directed her. A group of three or four men were gathered in front of the fire, each holding a drink. They seemed to be having a great time together. She picked out the one Jake was talking about and noted he seemed to have a roving eye as he kept track of every buxom waitress who passed him.

"Who is he?" she asked him.

"Hiram Bounce. He was actually one of my lieutenants at the beginning of the war." His face darkened. "He got caught sleeping with another officer's wife and he defected before his court martial. I thought he'd gone to the continent, but it seems he ended up here in Granvilli territory."

She nodded. He seemed the type. "He hasn't seen you, has he?"

"I don't think so."

"What do you think he'll do if he does?"

Jake shrugged. "Act like he's glad to see me and turn me in behind my back."

She sighed. "Then we'd better make sure he doesn't see you."

He turned and looked out, being careful to stay under his hood as much as he could. "That is getting harder and harder to imagine," he noted. "He and his group are edging closer and closer to the pathway in front of the door.. That's going to make getting out of here a problem."

She chewed on her lip for a moment, thinking it over. Luckily, there were enough people milling around in the room to give them cover for the time being. But Jake was right. There was no way he was going to be able to walk past the man to the doorway and not be noticed.

"What are we going to do?"

He shook his head, eyes troubled. "We can't stay here in this booth all night."

She nodded. "Maybe we could leave through the kitchen?" she suggested, but once they took a look at that route, they knew it wouldn't work. The way the waiters came barreling in and out through the swinging doors left no room for sneaking.

They ate their soup and it was wonderful, warming them from the inside while the heat of the fire warmed them on the outside. She fed Dede, which put her back to sleep. And then they watched Hiram and his friends laugh and joke and down more alcohol and wondered what to do.

Finally, Kim made a decision.

"Okay. How do I look?" She turned her face toward him and lifted her chin for examination.

"How do you look?" He gazed at her, puzzled. "Beautiful, as always. Why?"

"No, I'm serious. How do I look? My hair is all wet

and the snow has washed off all my makeup. So how bad is it?"

He shook his head, bemused by her words. "Kim, hasn't anyone ever told you that you have a luminous quality that shines right through all that?"

She smiled at him. "You're being very sweet, but not very helpful. I need to know if men are going to find me attractive."

He almost laughed aloud at that one. "In a word, yes."

"Okay." She began to gather things together. "You take Dede and just skulk around the outskirts of the crowd, going that way." She pointed it out. "Just lie low until I create enough of a distraction so that you can slip out through the door without anyone paying any attention to you."

He frowned. "Wait a minute. What exactly do you have in mind?"

"I'm going to make a brave attempt to be captivating enough to draw the men's attention. Wish me luck. In my bedraggled condition, I'm going to need it."

He frowned, looking stubborn. "I don't know. I don't like you putting yourself in jeopardy like that."

She gave him a look of pure exasperation. "Oh come on! I can do this. You don't think I can do anything, do you?"

He looked shocked at such a suggestion. "Of course I do. I know how talented you are. I just don't think you ought to waste those talents."

"Come on." She gave him a bright smile. "Let's do it."

Jake was still reluctant. He turned and glanced at the men over his shoulder.

"They've all had a few by now. What happens if they

don't let you go?" He turned back and looked at her. "What if they get a little too friendly, too fast?"

He had a point. The war had made everyone just a little bit harder, a little coarser, and a lot more difficult to deal with. But she put on a good front.

"I grew up in the castle. I know how to handle myself around a group of rowdy men."

He watched her for a moment and then a slow smile began to grow. "I imagine you do," he admitted at last, his gaze traveling so slowly over her face, it was almost caressing her cheek.

She smiled back. He'd done something to save her baby today. Now she hoped she could do something to help him.

Still, her heart was beating like a drum as she sidled up to the revelers. She'd talked big to Jake, but she wasn't sure just how rusty she might be at this sort of thing. She waited until Jake seemed to be at just the right angle across the room, holding Dede and getting ready to charge out the door, and then she made her move.

"Hey guys," she said, flouncing in the midst of the three and flashing her smile all around. "Is this a private party or can anybody join?"

Hiram was the only one she really focused on and he appeared startled, then immensely pleased.

"We've got special openings for girls as pretty as you, sweetheart," he said, leaning toward her. "What's on your mind?"

She gave him a flirtatious look. "My friend and I were just wondering how late you guys were going to be hanging around. We have an obligation we have to take care of, but if you're still going to be here in an hour or so, we thought we might come back and see what sort of celebration we can work our way up to."

All three men were practically drooling with anticipation by now.

"Any time, baby."

"Hey, if there's not a party when you get back, we'll make one happen for you."

But it was Hiram who noted something missing. "Where's your friend?" he asked, looking in the direction she'd come from and not seeing anyone interesting.

"She's...uh..." Kim craned her neck in the direction she wanted the men to look. "Well, she's back there somewhere. We were sitting at that booth."

From the corner of her eye she could see Jake beginning to sidle toward the doorway.

"Which booth?" Hiram began to frown, as though suspicious, and she felt her heartbeat stutter.

"That one," she said, pointing.

But Hiram was turning back. "I don't see her," he said, and his position was turned enough to see the doorway, just what she didn't want.

Jake was almost there. She had to do something fast.

"Well, come on," she said, reaching out quickly to take his arm and turn him away from the door. "Let's go look. She's got to be back here somewhere."

So now she had him by the arm and he was looking down at her as though he couldn't believe his luck.

"Hey, never mind. What do we need with her when we've got you?"

She knew her answering smile was a little shaky, but she gave it all she could. Jake had to be out the door by now. She risked a quick look over her shoulder.

Nope, he was still there. A woman with a large puff of red hair had stopped him, wanting to see the baby.

Kim whipped her head back around and went back to pretending to be fascinated by Hiram, but all she could think about was Jake, and silently, she was urging him to hurry.

All three men were saying things to her but she had gone beyond hearing them, so she just smiled and nodded and prayed Jake was gone by now. She held out as long as she could, then finally let herself steal another look.

Relief flooded her. He was gone.

"Hey, you know what?" she told her new friends. "I think my girlfriend has gone out and is waiting for me outside. I'm going to have to go. But we'll be back. You can count on that."

She flashed them each a quick smile and started for the door, hurrying, hoping.

But she wasn't going to get away so easily. Hiram was right by her side, slipping an arm around her shoulders and giving her a slimy smile that seemed to mean he was claiming her as his own.

"Hey, I'll go out with you," he said, hugging her closer than she liked as they left the room and went into the foyer. "I want to meet this friend. Is she as pretty as you?"

Her heart was in her throat. Now that her mission was accomplished, how was she going to shake this guy?

"Prettier," she said automatically, then glanced up at him and felt a shudder coming on. "But she's not for now, honey."

Pulling away from him, she pushed him back into the room.

"You just wait here. We'll be back."

Turning, she opened the door and the blast of cold air coming in from outside almost set her back on her heels. But even worse, Hiram was back again by her side, worse than a bad penny.

"I'm not going to risk losing you, now that I've found you," he said, and there was a steely glint in his eye as though he were warning her he didn't like all this kidding around. "Where is this friend of yours? In one of these cars?"

Kim looked out through the parking lot and her pulse raced. There was no sign of Jake. Where was he?

"Uh, I don't see her," she said, stalling for time and wondering a bit desperately how she was going to get Hiram to go back into the inn.

The door flew open again, and there were the other two men, each calling out to Hiram and Kim. Hiram turned back to yell a response at them and in that moment, they seemed to come together, each yelling something, like a scrum of young men pretending to be unruly puppies.

And at that moment, Jake came shooting out from behind a car and stopped the bike right where Kim was standing. He had Dede strapped to his chest and his hood down and there was no way anyone was going to recognize him. She jumped aboard, grabbing on to him, and off they went. Looking back, she could see that the men were just beginning to understand that she'd left them and seemed too befuddled to know what to do next. She held on to Jake more tightly and began to laugh.

But Jake wasn't laughing. "That was a little too close for comfort," he grumped.

Kim laughed again, exhilarated.

"It was a good thing they were stumbling all over each other or they might have noticed me waiting for you," he said. "As it is, I don't think they have a clue."

"You're right. I'm sure they thought my 'friend' was a surprisingly large, burly sort of girl piloting a motorcycle."

He looked back. "At least they don't seem to be following us. Probably couldn't find their car keys. We're lucky."

"You don't think we could have beat them on this trusty stead?"

"Not if any of them had anything that ran."

She laughed again, face into the cold wind. "That was fun. Let's find another inn and do it again."

Jake hunched over the handlebars and shuddered.

They drove on for another hour. The snow was letting up, but darkness was falling. Suddenly, Jake pulled off the road behind a small stand of trees and got off the bike, walking back toward the road and staring ahead.

"What is it?" Kim asked.

"I can't tell for sure, but it looks to me like that might be a roadblock up ahead." He pointed toward an area where there seemed to be a group of cars circling a set of floodlights.

"Why would there be a roadblock?" she asked, frowning.

He shrugged. "Who knows? Sometimes local militias get frisky and decide to take the law into their own hands. You never know." He turned and looked into the gathering gloom. "I think we'll head out into the open country for a while. You game?"

He looked at her. She looked up at him.

She had Dede again as they'd stopped and changed partners a while ago. But something about this trip was pulling the two of them closer together and forming a bond between them that she never would have expected.

"Sure," she said, feeling a little breathless from what she thought she saw in his eyes. "I'm ready for anything."

He smiled at her and reached out to touch her cheek. But only for a second, and then he was swinging back onto the bike, dousing the light, and they were off, leaving the road behind. But the tingle where he'd touched her was harder to lose.

"Hold on tight," he called back as they hit a rutted meadow.

The bike began to bounce like a bronco. She held on tight. Now, not only was it miserably cold and the going rough, her bottom was being punished like it had never been before. She felt as though a giant had taken her up and shaken her, then thrown her down in a way that made her bounce. For just a few minutes, she had some doubts about the survival of certain body parts.

But it didn't last much longer. He found a smoother path near a river, and then, finally, they were back on the road.

Jake stopped and looked back up the way they would have come. The lights of the blockade were just barely visible. They started off again, but he waited another couple of miles before he turned on his lights and it was a little spooky dashing through the darkness.

The wind had died down, and the snow was just light-as-a-feather flakes now, but it covered the countryside and coated every tree.

"Hey, remember what you said about it not snowing down at the lower levels?" he called back to her.

"Who, me?"

"Yes, you. You ready to revise that opinion?"

"Yes."

"Okay, just checking."

She sighed. "I've never seen it like this before. Isn't it beautiful?"

It was like a fairyland and eerily silent. The only sound was the bike as it putted along. A magic night, a magic journey. She sighed, wondering how she could so easily go from fearing him to being annoyed with him to being grateful—and now this. What was this exactly? She didn't know and she didn't want to think about it too hard. It was what it was, and it was obviously temporary. So it hardly mattered, did it? Whatever.

And then, finally, they reached the cliffs that Dorcher Cliffs was named for. The whole town spread out below them in lights, like a diamond necklace thrown carelessly upon an open beach. Many houses had lights strung, and some of the boats in the harbor were strung with lights, too. The entire town seemed to be aching to celebrate something.

Kim felt happy just looking down at her little town. She was home. They began to make their way down the winding road toward the cottage and she leaned forward and said, "You know what's coming up? Tomorrow is Christmas Eve."

"No kidding. I haven't been paying attention, I'm afraid."

"I know. You've been a little busy trying not to get killed lately."

"Exactly."

"I don't think you'll be in danger in Dorcher Cliffs," she said serenely. "So you can relax and enjoy the holiday."

She began to hum "White Christmas" against his neck.

He shook his head as she started to laugh. Suddenly she realized she'd been laughing a lot in the last few hours. She didn't laugh much these days. In fact, she thought she'd probably laughed more today with Jake than she had in all the months since the war began put together. It really seemed to be true that attitude was everything.

When they had started out from the city, she'd thought there was no way she could do this. But just being with Jake and listening to his silly jokes and feeling his concern and seeing how he looked at life as an adventure had changed everything. She had to remember that.

The cottage was small, just two bedrooms and a living room/kitchen combination, but there was a nice little yard with a covered patio that gave it a garden quality. The atmosphere was cozy. If you stopped and listened for a moment, you could hear the waves on the rocks, not far away.

This was where Kim had spent her early childhood, before her mother had been lured back to working and living in the castle despite the fact that it was under the Granvilli regime. Kim had gone with her and received early training in castle work, besides being accepted as the personal companion to Pellea.

Her mother had died before she turned eighteen, leaving her the cottage that they had used mainly for holidays in those last few years. Despite the fact that she didn't know many of her neighbors very well, she thought of Dorcher Cliffs as home and always had. Her mother's sister, Grace Day, had a small house down by the shore, but she'd lived in Paris for years and seldom visited.

Even after she'd been banished from the castle shortly after the war had begun and had fled here to have her baby, she'd kept to herself. Leonardo had never tried to find her here. She was pretty sure he'd gone on to other concerns. The good citizens of Dorcher Cliffs seemed to respect her need for privacy. They might leave a basket of freshly baked buns or a sack of home-grown fruit occasionally, but a smile and a few words of thanks seemed to suffice. They kept their distance but she never had a sense of animosity from them. All in all, it was a comfortable place to live.

As they drove in, she was surprised to see her aunt's house, with its old-fashioned Captain's walk around the roof peak, lit up as though someone was living there. Maybe her aunt was home for a visit. She would have to check that out.

The cottage smelled a little musty, as though no one had been in it since she'd left. She pointed out the fire-place to Jake and he quickly began to build a fire in the grate.

"That should take the chill out of the night," he said as he rocked back on his heels in satisfaction, looking at the results of his handiwork.

Kim smiled. It was so nice to have someone else there to help with things that had to be done. She re-alized, suddenly, how tired she was of being responsi-ble for everything. She changed poor Dede who'd been in the same diaper for hours, giving her a quick bath in warm water in the sink. She loved the water, bab-bling and cooing and splashing with her fat little hands, laughing as the bubbles rose. And then her little face registered a twinge of stabbing pain.

Kim could hardly stand it. She'd gone off to the city for six weeks to find relief for Dede and now she was back and not one step closer to finding help. As a mother, she was a class-A failure. She had to do something and do it now.

"What's it going to be, girl?" she asked herself softly. "What's it going to be?"

She picked her baby up and held her close, singing an old song that came readily to mind, and trying to use her love to heal her baby, even if only for the moment. That wasn't enough, but it was all she had tonight.

Carrying Dede out into the living room, she was still humming as Jake looked up and gave her a crooked smile.

"You know what, go take a shower," he said, reaching out for Dede. "That'll make you feel better. I'll take care of this little girl."

"Really?"

"Of course." The way he held her showed he knew what he was doing. "I've got a little bit of experience with this sort of thing, you know."

She remembered he'd had a baby of his own once. She smiled and did as he suggested. The shower restored her spirits. It was always a boost to feel clean and fresh.

She came out into the living room and found Jake in a rocking chair again, only this time it was a slender, rickety model her mother had used. Dede seemed to be sound asleep and Jake's head was back, but his eyes were open, if barely, and he gave her a slight smile as she got closer, though he didn't say a word.

She went on into the kitchen, opened the freezer and pulled out two sacks of frozen soup, popping them into the microwave. It was late and there was no time to fix a complete dinner, but a good soup was always welcome on a cold, snowy night. She hesitated, wondering if Jake would like some toasted bread with his soup, and was just about to go out and ask him, when she stopped herself.

No, doing that would be getting a little too friendly and accommodating. He would start to think she was trying to butter him up—either that, or falling for him. She had to keep her dignity and her distance. The trip through the snow had been one thing, but now that they had made it to their destination, better not to get too close.

Interestingly enough, Jake's thoughts were running along the same lines. He'd been sitting in the rocking chair holding this extremely loveable baby, enveloped in a cloud of baby happiness, and feeling nothing but peace and goodwill toward everyone—and it had to stop. This was not what he'd come here for. What did this have to do with the healing powers of vengeance?

It was Kim's fault. Something about her appealed to his senses—all of them—like no other woman he'd ever known. When he looked at her, he wanted her, wanted her in a deep, primal way that would make him take steps he knew he shouldn't take. And if that wasn't bad enough, he wanted her for more dangerous things as well. He liked talking to her. He liked the way her eyes lit up when she thought of something new. He wanted to touch her hair, her face. He liked looking at her, at the way laughter seemed to bubble up from inside her. Just catching sight of her made him feel warmer when it was cold. And when he looked at her, the urge to do something to make her happier began to fill the empty void he'd carried inside him for so long now. And that wasn't good. She wasn't the one to fill it.

But the worst thing was, he was feeling all these trai-torous emotions and urges around the woman who had been with Leonardo and had his baby—the last person on earth he could ever let himself love.

Love? Where had that word come from? His subconscious was dredging up old terms just because they seemed to fit his situation. But his subconscious was wrong. Love was not a word that would be relevant to him—never again.

No, this was just simple lust and hunger for human contact. That was all. And even that was too much. He held the baby as though she were the most precious thing in the world, and he knew, at this moment, she was. She couldn't help who her father was, so it had no bearing.

But Kim could help it. And he couldn't forget that.

"I like your cottage," he told her as she served up the soup at the dining room table. "It feels like a place one could call home."

"And I do." She took Dede from him and put her sleeping baby down in her little crib, then stood looking down at her.

Jake came up beside her, looking down as well. He was so close, his arm touched her shoulder. Why did that make her heart jump? She bit her lip, willing it to stop, but he'd turned his face toward her and she could feel his breath ruffling her hair. If she didn't watch out, her knees were going to buckle.

She looked up at him and he looked down at her and she felt like swooning. If he kissed her again, it would be different this time, and he had that look in his eyes. And no matter what she was telling herself, she knew she wanted it even more than he did.

She had to think fast—think of something that would stop this in its tracks.

"Jake," she began, her voice shaky, "tell me about your baby."

She felt his body stiffen. This was not a good question. But looking at his face, she decided she needed to know. It was time for him to talk about it, time for her to know the truth. And maybe it was time he let out some of his feelings. Who knew? She didn't get the sense that he had a lot of people he could talk to. If he needed someone, for now, let her be the one.

He was looking down at Dede again and it was soon apparent the sensual mood that had been developing between them had been blown to smithereens by her question.

"Not now," he said dismissively, though without turning away. He was too tired, suddenly, to argue, and yet too wound up to sleep.

And she seemed to feel the same way. But staying here, standing too close, letting emotions build, was out of the question.

"I'm going take my soup and sit on the couch and watch the fire until it burns out," she said. "It's that kind of night."

"I'll go with you," he said, but the tone of his voice warned her he might have more in mind than sipping soup.

Still, neither one of them spoke while they enjoyed their meal, letting the warm, nutritious comfort food do its work along with the fire. And even then, they sat for a few minutes and just soaked it in.

"Hey," Kim said at last, looking at him sideways. "I need to thank you. You saved Dede today, and you got us home, even though it took quite an effort. I owe you one."

He shook his head, staring into the fire. "Babies

are the most vulnerable ones in wartime. They can get caught in the crossfire so easily."

"Yes."

He turned and looked at her. "I've got to know, Kim. You've got to explain something to me."

A shiver went down her spine.

"What do you want to know?"

He turned back and stared into the fire for another minute. "I want to know why you think you belong with the Granvillis," he said softly. "I want to know why you have such animosity toward the royals."

Well, there it was. How was she going to explain this to him?

"Hey, there was just a war in this country, remember that? People had to make choices, pick sides."

His dark blue eyes looked haunted. "And what made you pick the side you went with, Kim?"

How could she explain her emotions at the time? She still didn't completely understand them herself. When Pellea had fallen for Monte, she'd helped her all she could. She hadn't thought twice. But later...

"A lot of people, even some in the castle, decided to back the invasion by the old DeAngelis royal family. I guess they had nostalgia for the old days or something. Or they wanted to return to the monarchy."

"But not you."

"No." She shook her head. "I grew up with the Granvillis, lived in the castle when the Granvillis were in charge, worked for them most of my adult life, and I stayed loyal." She said the words with fierce conviction, as though the harder she made her defense, the more valid it was. But glancing into his eyes, she had a feeling he wasn't buying it.

"Is that what you call it?" He said it softly, but his bitter streak was showing.

She gave him a resentful look, but she didn't say anything.

"Bad choice," he added.

That certainly put her back up. "You dare say that sitting right here in the heart of Granvilli territory?" She leaned back, watching at him with a sense of distance, as though she was trying to find a way to keep him at arm's length. "You shouldn't say things like that. You might be overheard, you know. Someone might turn you in."

His gaze was hard and pointed. "Someone like you?"

She turned away. Of course she wasn't going to turn him in and he knew it.

"Don't kid yourself, Kim. The Granvillis have had their day. They're done. Monte allowing them to stay on this side of the island while things are sorted out was a pity play. It's over."

Deep in her heart, she knew he was right. But there were reasons she couldn't accept it. At least not in front of him.

"Where was your loyalty to Pellea?" he went on. "You were best friends for years. Where did that friendship go?"

She closed her eyes, keeping her temper in check as much as she possibly could. She might ask where Pellea's loyalty had been, but he wouldn't understand. He hadn't been around when the world of Ambria had fallen apart and everyone had been forced to make their choices. What did he know of that? There was no point in even bringing it up.

"And now that we know you are the last royal baby," he went on in a matter-of-fact tone that she supposed was meant to help her start to accept it. "I think it's time you made some adjustments to your thinking." He turned in his seat so that he could see her more clearly. "Once you relax, you can start looking at the benefits of being a DeAngelis royal and maybe you'll even begin to be happy about it."

She'd taken all she could and she turned on him with a vengeance.

"I'm supposed to be happy about this?" she demanded sharply. "If this fairy tale you're trying to spin is true, do you realize what that does to my life? If you're right, you've just taken my world and ripped it apart. You've shown me that everything I believed to be true was lies. That the whole foundation of my life is a sham. That nothing is real. It's all an illusion. I'm a fading ghost lost in a funhouse of mirrors and cackling clowns."

He looked mystified at her reaction. "Kim, don't do this to yourself. This should be so easy."

"Easy? Easy?" She glared at him, her eyes shimmering with tears. "If all this nonsense is true, how am I supposed to go on living? It would mean that I've lost my mother. She was the woman who raised me. She was the one I loved. The only one who loved me." Angrily, she brushed her tears away.

"I never gave two figs for the DeAngelis king and queen. I never knew them, but what I knew of them was laughable. I mocked them time and again. And now you tell me they were my parents? How shall I make amends? Shall I jump off a bridge or s-s-omething?"

There was a lump in her throat and a sob tore into her last word.

"Kim," he began, reaching for her.

"Don't touch me," she snarled through clenched

teeth. Her fists were clenched and her eyes were a bit wild. "I'll...I'll scream or something."

"No, you won't," he said calmly. "Come here."

CHAPTER EIGHT

JAKE took Kim by the shoulders and pulled her closer. Despite all her fierce talk, she didn't do a thing to stop him. He held her face and kissed away her tears and murmured soft, comforting words that seemed to weave a magic spell around her. She closed her eyes and gave herself up to the feeling. When his lips touched hers, she kissed him back hungrily, begging for more.

She knew this was wrong and that she would regret it, but she couldn't stop herself. It had been so long since she'd felt the strong, protective arms of a man around her. She'd been so alone for so long. His mouth was hot and she accepted him eagerly, reaching up to dig her fingers into his hair and pull him ever closer. His hands flattened on her back and she arched toward him, aching for him to touch her breasts.

But he pulled his mouth away from hers, whispering something soft again, soothing her.

"Hush, Kim, take it easy," he said. "Don't let yourself get crazy. You're so tired…"

Pulling back, she stared at him, realizing he had just rejected her. She knew he felt the sensual tug between them as strongly as she did. So why would he do this?

Oh, of course. She knew exactly why.

"What is it?" she asked him evenly. "Did you just

remember I've been with Leonardo? Does that make me impossible to tolerate?"

His face registered shock and then a sort of stunned horror. That only made things worse. People always reacted like that once you'd put your finger on their secret.

"Kim." He grabbed her shoulders again, looking like he wanted to shake her. Then he calmed down, blinking rapidly. "Oh, Kim," he said, shaking his head. "This is really hard for you, much harder than I would ever have imagined."

Her return stare was a challenge. "So make it easier," she suggested.

He took a deep breath, then reached out to brush the tangled hair back off her forehead. "Okay," he said. "This is the best I can do. I'm going to batter you with facts."

She shrugged, unimpressed. "Batter away," she said coolly.

"Here goes. The reason I believe all this stuff you call nonsense and fairy tales, is because there is scientific evidence behind it all. Now I know that a lot of scientific material is subject to interpretation, and different scientists come back from the same facts with different opinions, but this stuff is DNA. It's like two plus two equals four. You can't argue with it."

"Whose DNA are we talking about?" she asked, frowning.

He didn't let her question sidetrack his narrative. "This research has been going on ever since the DeAngelis family took back the castle. Archivists have been doing surveys and sending out samples and all sorts of scientific things. The results have come back from all over the world, from everyone they could find who was even tentatively related to the DeAngelis royals. And then, more samples were taken from hair, from skin, from anything they could get. The rumors of a last baby had always been there, but no one had any proof, so they used DNA from anyone who was around in those days, and anyone affiliated with the castle since."

She was waiting anxiously now. This was like a mystery. She wanted to find out who the real killer was.

Or rather, the real last royal baby.

"And?"

"The results are in. It's official. They've found evidence that you belong in the DeAngelis family."

"What are you really saying?"

"I thought I was being quite clear. You're a DeAngelis, a princess of the realm. Now that there is a realm again."

She tossed her head back and forth, still anguished by this theory. "Sorry, but that just can't be right. Who else did they test?"

"Everyone. You are the only one who matched."

She thought fast. "Maybe they had a bad sample?"

"They had your hair from a brush in your room. They had your clothes. They had a sample of your blood from when you donated for the war effort. They had…"

"Okay, okay." She put her hands over her ears. She didn't want to hear any more.

"The other messengers that came. Didn't they try to explain it to you?"

"They told me gobbledygook and fairy tales that made no sense. I couldn't make heads nor tails of it."

He shook his head. "This is it, the straight scoop. You are the last of the DeAngelis family. You were born three days before the castle was burned by the Granvillis, twenty-five plus years ago."

"I know that part," she reminded him. "It's common knowledge. My mother was Lady Constance Day, lady-in-waiting to the queen. She hid her pregnancy as long as she could."

He took her face in his hands and smiled at her sadly. "No. Your mother was Queen Elineas. Lady Constance pretended you were hers so that the Granvillis wouldn't kill you."

She shook her head. It felt like she was doing it in slow motion, like she was watching herself from far away, and she saw her head move, and her hair spray out, but too slowly. It wasn't real.

"No," she said, and it sounded as though she were in an echo chamber. "No, that's ridiculous."

"It's true. Your DNA checks out." Reaching out he took her hand in his. He could see how this was affecting her. Somehow he had thought, despite everything, that this might make things easier for her. That she might cling to these facts in a changing, shifting world where the sand underneath your feet tended to leak away when you weren't paying attention. "Kim, it's true. It's science. You can't fight it."

"No." She was still shaking her head. "No. I don't want to be a part of the royal family. I was raised as a servant, taking care of a certain class, but free as a bird. My mother was a servant to the queen. I was a servant to the independent ladies of the citizens' regime. That was my place. Royalty wasn't even an issue. We didn't have any royals. We didn't want any. We hated the DeAngelis pretenders with their snooty ways. We were free, we were proud. We didn't need all that nonsense."

"That was then," he said simply. "Things have changed."

She stared at him. "They would never accept me

anyway," she whispered to him. "They didn't treat me like family when the chips were down. Why should I trust them now?"

He stared at her, aware there was something here he didn't understand. She'd been through things he couldn't even imagine. He didn't know what had happened, but he could see the shadows of the pain and anguish in her eyes.

"They hate me," she whispered, more to herself than to him.

"What are you talking about? They always accepted you. They love you."

"No." She knew things he didn't. Deep inside, she felt hollow and alone. "Not when the chips were down, they didn't. Leonardo..." But she wasn't going to talk about that.

He took her shoulders in his hands again and stared down into her face. "What about Leonardo?"

"Nothing." She shook her head. "Nothing."

He searched her eyes, but she wasn't going to give him any more. Still, he wanted to give her something. He had to help her get through this and come out the other side. And so he made her a promise.

"Listen to me, Kim. I want you to come with me to the castle. I know it will be for the best, for you and for Dede. But I'm not going to force you. The only way I'm going to get you there is if I can persuade you to come willingly."

He cringed inside. What was he doing here? His ace in the hole was always his physical prowess, the strong-arm stuff. His powers of verbal persuasion had never been strong. He had no gift of the silver tongue. And here he was, playing at the big table and putting all his money on the persuasion card. Wow. What an idiot he was.

But it was too late to turn back now.

"I swear to you, the only way I'm going to take you back is once I've persuaded you," he went on. "When you come with me, it will be of your own free will."

She stared at him. This was new. He hadn't felt this way before.

Could she believe him?

Maybe. Maybe not. She would have to take a leap of faith.

"Sleep on it," he suggested. "Let's go to bed."

It really was late. Their lack of sleep was finally catching up with them. Kim directed Jake to a bed he could use.

"You can sleep in my bedroom," she told him, pointing it out. "Right in there. I'll sleep on the little bed in Dede's room. I want to stay with her anyway."

He hesitated, looking down at her, then swallowed hard and turned away. It was better to start learning to avoid kissing her. No good could come of it anyway.

"Good night," he said over his shoulder.

He went into the room and started to unbutton his shirt, kicking off his shoes and reaching for the covers to pull them back. And there, on the newly uncovered pillow, lay a note. He took it up and held it to the light, but somehow, he already thought he knew who it would be from.

Kimmee my darling, it said in a large, masculine scrawl. *I have to see you. It's been too long. But I have to be careful. Watch for me on the holy day. L.*

He felt cold and then he felt hot fury and then he felt lied to. So she had no contact with him? Then what the hell was this? The thought of her with Leonardo almost doubled him over with pain. And then he was mad at himself for caring. He swore a blue streak, kicked a rug, and stormed out into the living room again.

"Kim," he said loudly. "I've got to talk to you."

She came out, dressed like an angel in that damn white nightgown again. He tightened his jaw and hardened himself.

"What is it?" she asked, suddenly anxious. "What happened?"

He handed her the note. She looked at it blankly, then began to read it. All the color drained from her face.

"Oh no," she moaned, looking around as though she expected him to jump out of the shadows. "He's coming. He's coming here!" She looked into Jake's face, her own eyes frantic. "We have to go. We have to get out of here. You don't know what he's like. I can't be here."

"He's not only coming," Jake said calmly, "he's been here."

She nodded, looking stricken. "I thought he didn't know about this place. I never thought he would come here. I…" She looked around as though for someplace to hide.

He watched her for a moment, and then he took her into his arms and held her close. He was convinced. She hadn't lied to him. And she didn't want to see Leonardo.

And yet, oddly enough, he did. This was playing right into his hands. The timing couldn't be better. If everything worked out the way it should, he would get his chance to make the man pay for what he'd done. Poor old Leonardo. He wouldn't know what hit him.

"Kim," he said, stroking her hair and holding her loosely, but still being careful of his ribs. "Calm down. I'm here. I won't let him do anything to you." He pulled back enough to see her face. "Has he hurt you in the past?" he asked, wondering at her reaction.

She looked at him, eyes wide, but she didn't answer. "I think we should go," she whispered. "He can't see Dede. What if he starts to want custody? He has all the power." She took Jake by his shirt and tugged. "Don't you see? We have to go."

"Doesn't he know about Dede?"

She hesitated, then shook her head. "I think he knows she exists, but he's never seen her, so she's just an abstract to him right now. But once he sees her in the flesh and realizes she's his...." Her face started to crumple, but she held it off. Still, her breathing was jagged.

"He said he was coming on the holy day. I assume he means Christmas."

She nodded. "I'm sure he thought he was being cryptic. As if a five-year-old couldn't figure out what he means."

"So we have over twenty-four hours," he said. "We need rest. And we need to plan." And he was going to have to find a way to explain to her that they needed to stay—because he needed to have it out with Leonardo.

She was shaking her head. "No. We need to go."

But as she looked up into his face, she realized that he wasn't really there standing with her any longer. Instead, he was back in some past time, viewing something horrible. For just a moment, she wondered what exactly it was that he was in danger of unleashing.

"You asked me earlier about my baby," he said. "About my family. Maybe it's time I told you." He glanced at her, then away again. "My baby and my wife were both killed in a market bombing over a year ago," he said flatly.

"Oh. Oh Jake, I'm so sorry. This damn war." She

saw the desolate look in his eyes and her heart broke for him.

He shook his head. It wasn't just the war. It wasn't a random act of violence. That marketplace was deliberately selected for punishment, and the man who meted it out was the man Kim had selected to father her child, Leonardo Granvilli. The ruler of the exiled realm.

"I've never told anyone the whole story. Not even Pellea." He looked down and touched her cheek. "But I'm going to tell it to you."

"Why? Why me?"

"I think you'll understand that by the end."

She nodded reluctantly, not sure why he put it this way, as though once she'd heard his story, she would assume some responsibility for it. She wasn't sure she wanted that job.

"Okay."

"I'm going to start way back at the beginning. You know that I grew up away from Pellea and my father, away from the castle, and mostly, away from Ambria. But I went to schools where other Ambrians went." He smiled faintly. "In my own way, I've always been a patriot."

She led him to the couch again and they sat down, closer together this time.

"I never met Pellea until we found each other in Hungary where she'd gone to find medical care for our father. I heard she was there and I went to see them both. It was amazing how suddenly that old family tie reasserted itself with a vengeance. Pellea and I looked in each other's eyes and we felt the connection immediately. It was like looking in the mirror. I knew who she was and she knew who I was. Instant rapport."

Kim frowned and looked away. She'd felt that way

with Pellea at one time. How could she warn him to beware? It wouldn't last.

Or maybe it would for him. After all, he was a real brother, not a pretend sister like she'd been.

"I got closer to my father," he was saying. "I met Monte. I met the whole crew and we all got along famously."

"They're all very charming," she said with a pang of memory.

"Yes. I liked them a lot."

Of course. She'd liked them, too.

"So you decided to throw your lot in with the new rebels," she said, a trace of her sarcasm showing. "You got yourself involved in the invasion of Ambria."

"Yes. I signed on to their cause. I thought what had happened to the royal family when the Granvillis took over and burned the castle and killed the king and queen was outrageous and deserved punishment. I was all for the invasion."

"And yet, your father…"

"I can't be held accountable for what my father did," he interjected sharply. "I can only offer my own opinions."

She nodded. She accepted that. "Bad things happen in wars," she said, sounding like an automaton.

"Oh yes, they do indeed. But we invaded Ambria and we got the castle back. It all happened so fast, even we were surprised at how immediate our success was. We came in from the sea and we drove them back and they went."

Kim looked down and realized her fingers were trembling. He remembered this as a time of triumph. She remembered the panic, the mad rush to find transportation away from the castle, the way everyone turned

on everyone else. She'd been accused of spying for the
DeAngelis royals, of all things. There was actually talk
of jail time while charges were developed. Instead—
Leonardo stepped in. And that was even worse.

At first, she'd thought he really wanted to help her.
What a fool she'd been.

"And at that time," Jake was going on, "we thought,
well, if it's this easy, maybe there doesn't have to be
any more killing. Maybe we can do this through talk
and negotiation. Maybe it could all be over."

Kim's smile was jaded. She wasn't that naive. She'd
seen too much. "Not in this lifetime."

"Maybe not." He shook his head. "At any rate, it just
so happened that I knew Leonardo."

"Really?" Yes, he'd mentioned that before. "Where
did you meet him?"

"We were at Eton together, but only for one term. We
were rivals in everything from sprinting to debating."
He laughed shortly. "We hated each other even then."

"I can imagine." By now she had curled into a ball
of instant misery, but he didn't seem to notice.

"But having the advantage of this connection, I tried
to contact him. I wanted to help the DeAngelis royals.
From my perspective, I find them a fine set of people
who want the best for this country."

"By 'this country', I assume you mean a united
Ambria."

"Of course."

She sniffed and he gave her a look.

"I sent him messages. He had his man respond, but
he didn't answer himself. Still, I thought we'd developed a line of communication. I offered to meet him
in a coffee house on the square in Tristan, just off the
Novio marketplace. A fairly neutral area."

She nodded. She knew that place. And she was afraid she also knew what was coming next.

"I told him where I would be sitting and that I would be open to setting a foundation for the beginning of negotiations. I tried to give him a broad opening and a sense that there would be a place for him in the new Ambria if he wanted to lay down arms and join us."

She rolled her eyes. "I can just imagine his response to that."

"He agreed to meet."

She shrugged. Even that was surprising, from what she knew of the man. "But did he actually show up?"

"No." He was silent for a long moment, and when he spoke again, his voice was hard and steely. "And here's the really stupid part. I let my wife and baby come along with me."

She sat up, staring at him with her mouth open. "What?"

"Not into the coffee house," he explained quickly. "But to the marketplace. Cyrisse had a good friend who ran one of the high-end shops and she went to visit her while I waited for Leonardo."

"So you treated this like a day at the mall?" she said, aghast. He couldn't be this naive. Here she'd thought he was so tough and worldly wise.

"You had security guards, didn't you?" she asked, shocked at such casual disregard for human safety.

The Granvillis were not known for their compassion. In fact, they were pretty much known for murder and mayhem. And she was sure Jake quickly found that out.

"Of course. And so did my wife." His groan was more angry than sad. "A lot of good that did."

Kim began to get a hint of what was coming and her blood ran cold.

"Oh no," she whispered.

"Yes. I was so stupid. So inexperienced in dealing with evil. I really thought there was a chance we could get together and begin work on restoring Ambria to what it deserved to be. I thought Leonardo would be willing at least to listen."

"But no."

"No."

They were silent for a long moment, each thinking sad thoughts.

"A little girl?"

"Yes."

"How old was she when...?"

"Six weeks."

"Oh my God. So young."

He couldn't speak for a moment, and when he did, his voice broke often. "So young, so new, so bright, so full of promises...gone in an instant."

She waited a moment before she spoke again. "What exactly happened?"

"They bombed the marketplace. I'm sure they meant to get me, but they were off a bit. They got my life instead and destroyed it in front of my eyes. I suppose, in their view, that was just as good."

She nodded, knowing that the people who set the bomb didn't care. They just wanted mayhem. They wanted blood. They didn't know much about sitting in a coffee house and having a nice polite discussion about power and who was going to get it. All they knew were weapons and killing.

"And you blame Leonardo."

His was voice was like ground glass. "I want him dead."

She nodded. If he only knew how close his senti-
ments were to her own.

They sat silently for a few minutes, mulling over
what he'd just told her.

Then he seemed to have himself together again and
he turned and looked at her.

"So now you tell me," he said, studying her pretty
face. "How is it that you ended up with Leonardo? How
did you manage to screw up your life to that extent?"

She looked at him and weighed how much she wanted
to tell him. "Okay, here's how it was," she started off.
"It was right before the invasion began that…that…
Well, there was a lot going on in the castle at the time.
Leonardo's father was dying, leaving him in charge, and
he had to fight off a lot of other factions who wanted
the control and the power that looked up for grabs to
them. But Leonardo stuck to his guns and he won out
over all the others."

"In the meantime, Pellea was gone. She'd left with
her father to search for medical help for him in Europe.
At least that was the reason she gave when she got permission to leave. But she didn't come back and soon
we heard that she was with Crown Prince Monte."
She winced, remembering that time. "Leonardo went
crazy. He'd pretty much forgotten about her while he
was in his power struggle, but now that it was over, he
wanted her back. He knew he was about to be invaded
by Monte's forces. He couldn't stand to think the woman
who was supposed to have married him was now with
his enemy."

Jake snorted. "What a loser."

She shrugged. "He was insanely jealous at the time,
and when he couldn't have Pellea, he decided…" Did
she really want to tell him about this? Oh, why not? He

would learn it all eventually. "He decided I would do in her place, at least until he could get his hands on her again."

Shock echoed through Jake's crystal-blue gaze. "What are you saying, Kim? Did he force you...?"

Her dark eyes were haunted with regrets and memories. "I'm not going to talk about that. Not ever. I'll just tell you that it was a very difficult situation. And it lasted too long. I wanted desperately to get out of it. I sent letters to anyone I could think of. And when the DeAngelis forces invaded, and so quickly won back the castle, I sent messages to Pellea directly, asking her to intervene and get Leonardo to let me go."

"But?"

She steeled herself. This was one time she wasn't going to allow her voice to break. No emotion. Just the facts. "No one ever came. No one rescued me. No one cared."

She didn't want to think about the details, the days she spent pacing the room where he had her locked away, how desperately she looked through the messages they allowed her to receive, how she prayed and prayed that someone would come. And the nights... Best not to think about them.

"Did she ever get the messages?"

She gave him a look. "I sent them with a very trusted envoy. I'm sure she got them. She just didn't answer. I guess at that point, she was just too busy becoming queen."

He frowned. This was something he hadn't heard about. He was going to have to look into the truth of this. He knew how much his sister loved Kim. He couldn't imagine that she would have ignored a cry for help from her.

"So you stayed with Leonardo for an extended period of time."

"It seemed like forever."

"Did you...love him?"

"Love him?" She looked almost physically sick.
"Love had nothing to do with it."

Jake felt a little sick himself. "What did he do to
you?" he asked, his voice harsh.

She avoided his gaze. "I told you that was something
I'm not going to talk about."

He nodded.

"I spent a lot of time hoping someone would pay
some attention. And then suddenly, the DeAngelis family was back and they were in charge of the castle and
everybody on their side was celebrating. They were in
all the papers, all the magazines. They were tooting
horns and singing songs, and they never seemed to remember that I had ever existed."

She took a deep breath. "I felt more than betrayed.
I felt erased. Like everything I'd ever done was gone,
forgotten, no longer important. Everyone I'd ever loved
had just turned their back on me and didn't care. That
I was only important when I was useful."

He looked at her, expecting to see tears, but her voice
was hard as diamonds and her eyes were dry and filled
with anger. He wanted to do something to make her feel
better, but what could he possibly do? Maybe get her to
look at this in a broader perspective, see it in the larger
scheme of things.

"But Kim, don't you see?" he tried. "That's the way
it always is in life. People are basically self-centered and
see the world through a selfish lens. They often don't
think about others until their own needs have been ful-
filled."

She gave him a scathing look. "You can say that all you want, and I know it's often true, but that doesn't make it any better. It still hurts."

He stared at her, at a loss for words. He wanted to grab her and kiss her pain away, but he knew that wasn't going to work. It might make him feel a whole lot better, but it probably wouldn't do much for her.

"Go back to the castle," he said shortly. "Talk to Pellea. I'm sure you two can work things out. I know how much she cares for you. There has to be some reason."

"Forget it."

He looked at her, a bit exasperated. "You may not be able to forgive those who have hurt you, but your baby shouldn't have to pay for that."

"Oh no," she said quickly. "You're absolutely right."

She looked at him, realizing they had left his own heartbreak behind to talk about hers. And really, his was so much worse.

Gazing at him, she was suddenly filled with a warmth she didn't expect. Here he was trying to make her feel better. And what had she done for him? She'd criticized his handling of the meeting that had resulted in his beloved family dying. Nice person she was.

"Jake," she said, getting his attention. "Stay still."

Leaning toward him, she kissed his warm mouth. His lips parted in surprise and she took advantage of him, flicking her tongue inside and teasing him. She heard a growl, deep in his throat, and then he was kissing her back, wrapping her in his arms and leaning her back onto the couch. She began to laugh, and he kissed her harder. He tasted like red wine and he felt like a gladiator, all muscle and hardness. Except for his mouth. And for a moment, she couldn't get enough of it.

But they both knew the dangers they were courting, and they drew back easily, laughing in each other's eyes and pulling away. It was late. They needed sleep.

But Kim was glad she'd provoked a little romance for the evening. And now she had a kiss to build a dream on.

CHAPTER NINE

DEDE woke up early, and that meant that Kim woke up early as well. Kim got up to feed her and play with her, so she had time to think over what had happened the night before. Despite all the stories and experiences they had related to each other, all the emotional turmoil, it all meant little when you got to the bottom line.

And the bottom line was Dede. She needed to see a real doctor, and that was all that mattered. Kim was resigned. She was going to the castle. Getting the menacing note from Leonardo had put the seal of certainty on it. There was nothing else to do, and no other way left to do it. She would have to face Pellea and all her old friends—the ones who had turned their backs on her.

But she wouldn't play their game. She was going to tell them that even if the DNA said she was a DeAngelis, that didn't make her a princess. She didn't want to be one. They could put her on the lists and put her picture on the wall and announce her name at balls—but she wouldn't appear in person. No participation awards for Princess Kimmee. She had other things to do with her life.

Still, she had to admit, the things Jake had said were eating away at her tough-girl stand. Maybe there were explanations for what had happened. Maybe she shouldn't have been so quick to decide she'd been left behind because no one cared about her. Maybe her resentment had been simmered in too thick a sauce of self-pity. Just a little.

She wasn't really as frightened anymore at the prospect of seeing Leonardo as she had been the night before. Just the thought that he'd been inside her little cottage gave her the creeps, but there was nothing for it but to move on. What was done was done. Time to pick up the pieces and find a new way.

Oh, who was she trying to kid? She was still terrified that the man would try to take Dede from her. And that was a big part of the reason she'd decided to go to the castle.

She looked around. She loved her cottage but she was afraid it might be a long time before she would be able to come back to it.

She had Dede in her highchair and was feeding her creamed peaches when she heard the front door open. She jumped up, her heart in her throat, sure it was Leonardo arriving early. What was she going to do?

"Hey, anybody here?"

It was Jake's voice she heard, and she let the air out of her lungs with a rush, half laughing, half annoyed, but completely filled with relief as she turned to greet him.

"I thought you were still asleep," she said, her hand over her heart.

"I got up early, so I went out in the snow." His smile was full of mischief. "I've got a surprise for you."

"What have you got?" she cried.

He reached back out the door and brought in a little cone-shaped tree with a wooden base already hammered on.

"I figured, as this is Dede's first Christmas, she needed a little Christmas tree. So I went up to the woods and cut her one."

It was perfect, a small conifer shaped exactly like what was needed. He set it in on the table and reached into the pockets of his coat, pulling out items he obviously planned for decorations.

"We have here some red berries I found in bushes growing along the side of the road," he said. "And some little pine cones that look almost golden. In the right light. And a garland of holly-like vine that was growing down by the stream."

"Perfect," she said, her eyes shining. "I'll get some yarn to make hangers for them."

"And I have one more thing," he said, reaching back into his pocket. "Just for Dede." He pulled out a little mechanical Santa Claus, all dressed in red with a big white beard. "Look Dede. What do you think of this?"

The baby laughed and clapped her hands with delight. Jake made the little Santa dance for her, bringing on peals of laughter.

"Where did you get that?" Kim asked him, loving the way he made her baby laugh.

He gave her a sheepish look. "To tell you the truth, I stole it," he admitted.

Her jaw fell. "What?"

"Well, there aren't too many stores open at this time of the morning."

"But to steal it! Where? What did you do?"

"It was in a yard over near the church."

"Right in front of the church you stole something!"

He was laughing at her and he reached out and

touched her golden hair. "Will you listen? It was in a yard, half buried, as though kids had been playing with it yesterday and forgot it when the snow started. So I picked it up and brought it home for Dede to see."

"Jake!"

"I'm taking it back," he said defensively.

She had her hands on her hips. "When?"

He shrugged. "When Dede is tired of it."

She was exasperated with him, but still, she started to laugh. "Next thing you know, one of the town elders will be banging on the door, wanting your head on a spike. You can't do these things in small towns. Someone is bound to have seen you."

"Don't worry. They'll never connect it with you. I made a lot of maneuvers on my way back here."

"Wonderful. I'll bet you looked guilty as all heck from the lookout area on the town hall bell tower."

He gaped at her. "Why would anybody be up there at this time of the morning?"

"Trust me. Someone saw you. They always do."

She began to work on hanging the home-grown ornaments and he watched her, enjoying her ready smile and the way her eyes flashed with humor at the slightest provocation. Was it just the proximity that was making him like her this much? Was it just the heightened excitement of the journey they were on?

Memories of Cyrisse, his wife, flickered into his thoughts, and he frowned, wondering if this was a betrayal of her and all she'd meant to him. They had known each other for years and been good friends, then, briefly, lovers. When Cyrisse told him she was pregnant he'd been surprised, but willing to take on the responsibility of a family. It seemed to be the right time for it, he'd argued with himself, and though the two of them had never been particularly passionate partners, love would probably grow out of shared responsibilities and experience. When she was killed, he'd mourned her, but it had been the baby, little Jessica, whose loss had created the hole in his heart.

All things being equal, he knew he could fall hard for Kim. She engaged his senses like no other woman he'd ever known. She filled his head and his heart in ways he had never imagined. How easy it would be to pull her into his life—if only she didn't have ties to Leonardo.

And despite everything she said, despite the way she really did seem to fear him, those ties still existed. It would take more than the short time he'd known her to analyze how deep emotions ran between them. Had she ever loved the man? That would be hard to believe, but people did strange things at times.

"I think we should go soon," she was saying as she hung the last spray of red berries on the little tree.

"Go where?" He looked up, coming out of his reverie.

"To the castle." She was biting her lip, looking worried.

"Are you sure?"

"Yes. Things have changed."

"And you want to go now?"

"Yes. As soon as possible."

He looked out the window, grimacing. How was this for irony? She was finally ready to go to the castle just when he had a chance to come face-to-face with Leonardo. A part of him wanted to rebel, to tell her the trip to the castle could wait until after....

After what? After he had a chance to deal with the

man? Right here in front of his child and that child's mother? That wasn't going to work.

Didn't they say vengeance was a dish best served cold? This one was going to be icy. But it would be served. It was just a matter of time.

"How about going right after lunch?" he suggested. "Then we'll reach the border about nightfall. That's a good time to get across without being seen."

"Sounds good. I'll start getting things ready."

She spent a half hour cleaning the kitchen, then pulled out the ingredients for cookies—big, meaty peanut butter cookies with chocolate chunks—for the trip. Soon the kitchen was filled with delicious cookie-baking smells.

Jake went to take the little Santa back to its yard without too much prodding and Kim was taking the last batch of cookies out of the oven when the doorbell rang. Kim froze, sure this had to be bad luck. Either that nosy village elder had come calling, or Leonardo was early. Her heart pounding, she looked out the window—and to her surprise, found her mother's elderly sister from Paris at the door.

"Aunt Grace!" She hurried to let her in. "It's wonderful to see you. Please come in."

It had been years since she'd seen her aunt, who spent most of her time living with her new husband in Paris. She looked lovely, her skin smooth, her coloring rosy, her ensemble chic and stylish. This was the way Grace had always been. Kim's own mother had tended more toward hair in a tangle and a dress that didn't quite fit, but her sister was interested in finer things.

"You look amazing," Kim said, shaking her head at her beautiful aunt.

"That's because I live in Paris," Grace said with a

lovely laugh. "We do pay more attention to appearances there."

"Well, you've certainly learned to be a Parisian then, haven't you?"

"In my way."

"How long are you staying?"

"We just came for the holiday. Jacques—my new husband. He's so young, you know, and I wanted to show him where I used to live when I was his age."

"I see," said Kim, somewhat taken aback. "Well, if you're around at the end of the week, maybe we can get together. I'm afraid I must make a trip to…well, away, for a few days."

"Ah, what a shame. Well, I'll stop by again before we leave to see if you've come back. I'm hoping we can connect and do something together."

"I hope so, too."

As her aunt turned to go, Kim thought of a question she could ask her.

"Aunt Grace, maybe you can help me with something. There have been rumors swirling lately, rumors about my background."

"Oh dear."

"Because of my connection with the castle."

"Of course."

"And…well, I'd like to know the truth."

Grace laughed. "Be careful, my dear. As you grow older, you may find that the truth is something best hidden from public view."

"Oh no," Kim said, reacting reflexively with a saying she'd always heard. "The truth will set you free."

"They lied to you, my dear. The truth will often make you cry." She patted her shoulder. "But ask away. I'll see what I can do to clear up any false rumors."

Kim took a deep breath and decided she might as well come straight out with it. "Was your sister, Constance, really my mother?" she asked in a rush.

Grace blinked, surprised at the question. "You see, this is just the kind of thing one really doesn't want to get into."

"I just need to know. They...they're saying someone else was my mother and...and..."

"I can't tell you for sure. I wasn't living with Constance at the time. But I did visit her about a month before you were born and she didn't seem pregnant to me."

"Oh."

"Now, she may have been very clever at hiding it. Who knows? But when she came back home with you in her arms, we were quite surprised."

"I see."

"And as you know, Constance was not the sort of woman to have an affair. In fact, she was pretty vocal about women who did so." Grace made a face. "Even when that woman was her own sister."

"Oh, Aunt Grace!"

Kim reached out to comfort her, but Grace laughed. "We all make our own choices in life, darling. And we learn to bear the consequences. I've lived a wonderful life. But so did Constance. And she never said a word about who your father might be."

Kim nodded. Grace's information filled in a few gaps, but only marginally. "I think you've given me my answer," she said anyway.

"Have I, dear? I hope it doesn't make you cry," Grace said, turning toward the door.

"No, don't worry about that. I've cried enough for one lifetime."

Grace turned back as though she'd forgotten to say something. She hesitated, then reached out and patted Kim's cheek. "I hope you know that Constance loved you as deeply and truly as any mother ever would," she told her earnestly.

"Yes. Yes, I do know that." Kim kissed the older woman and smiled, eyes misting with tears. "But thank you for reminding me. I loved her, too."

Once Jake got back from returning the Santa, they both seemed to feel a sudden urgency to get going.

"I've agreed to go with you to the castle," Kim told him. "Just don't give me any of that malarkey about being royal."

"I won't say a word," he said. "The motorcycle isn't great for conversation anyway."

She made a face at him and frowned. "I don't suppose we could borrow a car from someone."

"We'd have to abandon it in a ditch when we get to the border."

She sighed. "I guess borrowing is out."

It felt strange piling on top of the rickety bike again. Most of the sense of adventure she'd had by the end of the ride the day before seemed to have evaporated. It didn't help that Dede was fussing and Jake had a hard time getting the bike started. But once they were back on the road, it wasn't so bad. It wasn't snowing but the air was crisp and cold. They cruised along the coast, enjoying the scenery, then turned inland, heading for the best border crossing, aiming at an arrival near dusk.

"Why is it that you can't find a policeman anywhere in this country but the checkpoint is full of soldiers?" she asked in exasperation.

"They're trying to keep people from deserting a sinking ship," he said. "Plus, from what I've heard, the soldiers haven't been paid and this is their way of making a living. They shake down travelers."

"Lovely."

"Granvilli honor in action," he said, trying to keep from sounding too bitter.

"It's Christmas Eve," she had reminded Jake before they left. "Let's hope some of them are distracted by that in itself."

"You expect the Granvilli border guards to be off singing Christmas carols?" he asked with a grin.

"You never know," she said defensively. "They might be putting on a pageant."

"Maybe we could be the wise men," he said, mocking her gently.

"Right. I'm sure they'd like that."

But it did feel momentous, traveling across the country like this, planning to illegally cross a border. Her heart was pounding harder than usual, especially when she remembered she would probably be meeting with Pellea in just a few hours.

Night was falling when Jake pulled over to the side of the road. "Look up ahead," he told her. "See the lights? That's the checkpoint. We're going to ditch the bike and walk in, but we won't be far from the lights. Unfortunately, we have to go in really close, close enough that they might see us. But it's the best place to cross, so we'll have to risk it."

She got off the bike and put Dede down while she helped him hide the bike in a gully, covering it with leaves. Then they gathered their things and Jake took the baby and they started walking, staying in the thickest brush they could find.

"Come this way," Jake whispered, leading her into a

stand of pines, then doubling back through lower shrub-
bery. He began to walk more slowly, more carefully,
and she followed suit. She could see the lights coming
nearer and nearer, but the first time she heard a man's
voice, sounding just a few feet away, she jumped and
had to bite down hard to avoid a small scream of surprise.

Jake motioned for her to come through and then hun-
ker down where he was.

"This is closer than I expected," he whispered. "If
they tried hard, they could see us. The brush cover is
pretty thin."

She nodded, not daring to say anything aloud. She
could hardly believe how near they were. She could see
faces plainly and hear snatches of what was said. She
was afraid to even breathe.

"I think we'll be okay as long as Dede doesn't cry,"
Jake whispered.

She looked down at her baby. Wide eyes met hers.

"Oh boy," she breathed. This would be touch and go.
When Dede was awake, noise was her business.

"Look."

A black sedan with tinted windows was approach-
ing the border guards and they went into readiness.
The driver slowed the car to a stop and said something
out the window. The border guard seemed to disagree,
shaking his head as he looked at the credentials he'd
been handed.

They held their breaths, knowing this might be the
perfect time to make a run for it, but hesitating.

And then the back window of the car opened and a
tall man leaned out, barked an order and got immediate respect from the guard.

Kim gasped and grabbed Jake's arm. "Leonardo!"

But he already knew that. He stared at the man. Everything in him went cold and his gorge rose. Leonardo. He pushed Kim's hand away and tensed, adrenaline flowing. If he called out, would Leonardo meet him halfway? Would he take the challenge? Would he know why it had come to him? No matter. The man needed to pay. He dropped his backpack and took a step toward the checkpoint.

Kim stared at him for a split second and then she realized what he was doing. "No!" she whispered, throwing herself in his way, physically holding him back. "No, you can't."

They stared at each other. She saw the look in his eyes and it scared her. He wanted revenge and he was like a machine programmed to get it.

"No!" she whispered again, shaking her head.

They looked back at the car. The window was rolling up and the car was beginning to move. The guard stood back, saluted and let them through. In a moment the car was gone, most likely on its way to Dorcher Cliffs.

Kim drew air into her lungs. It felt as if she'd been holding her breath for a long, long time. Jake was swearing and shaking his head. She looked at him and shook her head, as well.

"Are you crazy?" she whispered at him. "Come on. We have to get over that border."

Jake nodded. He knew she was right. But he was shaking with anger, with hatred. If ever a man deserved a good killing…

Was he going to get it? Not today. But soon.

A quarter of a mile later, and they were solidly in DeAngelis territory. Jake took out his cell phone. It worked! Quickly he called the castle and ordered a car to come out and get them.

"Hey," he said, smiling happily at Kim. "We're home."

The castle rose above the darkness and the mist like a legendary, magical place where fairy tales and stories of King Arthur were born. A lump rose in Kim's throat. She hadn't expected to feel this way, but there it was. The place she'd once called home. She still loved it.

Memories surged all around her—good and bad. Tears welled in her eyes and she couldn't seem to get rid of them.

The car dropped them at the side entrance and they were waved in by guards. The corridors looked so familiar, though the people working there were complete strangers on the whole. Kim stayed close to Jake. Funny—she was the one who had lived here for so long, but he was the insider now.

He led her to an elevator, and then to a familiar large wooden door.

"Pellea thought you might like to use the chambers she lived in all those years you and she were like sisters. And if you decide to stay, they can be renovated to suit your needs."

Pellea's courtyard! She'd always loved the place. It was a garden retreat built right into this side of the castle. There was a small lush forest open to the sky, along with a greenhouse garden filled with flowers. The surrounding rooms—a huge closet filled with clothes and a small sitting room, a neighboring compact office stacked to the ceiling with books, a sumptuously decorated bedroom—each room opened around the courtyard with the same French doors, making the living space a mixture of indoors and outdoors in an enchanting maze of exciting colors and provocative scents. It was a space fit for a princess. Walking into it was like walking into an enchanted place.

Was it a bribe?

"Where are you staying?" she asked Jake, holding on to his arm as though it were keeping her afloat.

"I have a suite on the other side of the wing." He looked down at her and at the way her fingers were digging into his arm. "But I'll stay with you as long as you need me."

"Need you?" She blinked and looked up at him, not sure what he meant.

He covered her hand with his. "I can see how tense you are. You're scared to death."

"No, I'm not." But the shivers that kept coming up in waves through her body gave lie to her claim.

"You've got a lot to worry about," he told her. "I know that. If you want, I'll go with you to face Pellea."

"Will you? Really?" She was embarrassed. She wasn't usually such a coward. But the way she felt about Pellea went right to the core of her being, and this fight with her had been tearing her apart. The thought of having Jake there to steady her, to act as her backup, to lean on, if need be, brought her such a sense of relief, she knew she had to have him with her.

A young woman, evidently assigned to be a nanny for Kim, stood waiting and ready to help, but Kim didn't want to hand Dede over to anyone until she was secure and sure of just what was going to happen.

"Thanks," she said with a quick smile. "Maybe a little later."

"Anytime, miss. Just ring and I'll come quickly."

"Thank you."

It made her a little nervous to have someone ready to wait on her. That was her job!

"You go ahead and get settled in," Jake told her. "I'll go see if Pellea is ready to see you."

"That's right. She is the queen, isn't she? She probably has to see all kinds of people all the time."

"Yes, she does. But I know she'll make time for you whenever you're ready."

She nodded and took a deep breath. "I'm ready. Just let me wash up and…"

"And I'll be back to escort you over in a few minutes," he said. He used his bent index finger to lift her chin and smile into her face.

"Everybody loves you here," he reminded her. "No need to stress."

She nodded like someone who wasn't convinced, but she watched him go and turned back to her baby. The one solid feature of her life. Dede was all that mattered. It was for Dede that she was here.

Taking a deep breath, she got on with it.

Pellea was excited when she saw her brother come into her reception room. She excused herself from the local energy minister who was conferring with her, and came to Jake and took his hands as he kissed both her cheeks.

"Well?" she asked. "Is she here?"

"She's here." He frowned. "She's in a bit of a fragile state, though. Be gentle. Be kind."

Pellea looked insulted. "Am I ever anything else?" Then her gaze sharpened. "Why do you care so much?" she probed, pretty sure she already knew the answer to her question.

He hesitated and she laughed, her eyes sparkling with delight.

"Never mind. What I want to know is, has she told you why she wouldn't come back to us?"

He nodded, considering just what to say. "She feels betrayed."

Pellea frowned. "In what way?"

"She felt abandoned and forgotten. She reached out and no one responded."

Pellea shook her head thoughtfully. "We were trying to get in touch with her the whole time."

"You'd better find a way to prove it to her. She's pretty bitter."

"Oh, I hate to think of how hurt she must have been." Pellea was distressed. "But don't worry. I think I've got some evidence that will convince her."

His frown was dark and brooding. "I hope it's good."

"And you?" she asked. "How are you getting along with her?"

He looked surprised. "Fine. And none of your business."

She laughed. "Oh. Good."

"Now about the baby," he said earnestly.

"Yes. I've heard Kimmee is very worried about her, but isn't sure what is wrong."

"Exactly. She's been searching for a decent pediatrician for months with no luck."

Pellea nodded. "I've already sent for the best we have. It's a bit of a struggle, being the holidays and all, but I think I've got four who have promised to show up by tomorrow afternoon. If they can't figure out what's wrong, we'll send to the continent."

"Great. That will be a big relief to her."

"And to you."

"But I need to warn you. I'm going to have to go back over to the other side."

"Why?"

"I know where he is."

"Who? Leonardo?"

"Yes."

She gripped his arm. "Jake, let the guard take care of it. There's no reason for you to risk your life."

He covered her hand with his own. "Pellea, there's every reason for me to do it. I have to do it. I'll go before dawn, the day after Christmas."

"At least take a few of the guard with you."

He shook his head. "I'll make better time on my own." Leaning forward, he kissed her again. "Don't worry. I'll be careful. I'll be safe. And I'll be back."

CHAPTER TEN

Jake returned in a few minutes with Dede in his arms and Kim in tow.

"Here she is."

Pellea came forward, her heart beaming from her dark eyes. "Kimmee! Oh my darling Kimmee! I feel like I've waited forever for this."

Kim was looking a bit stiff, but Pellea ignored that and threw her arms around her. "I'm so glad to see you."

"I'm…I'm glad to see you, too."

After a few seconds of hesitation, Kim hugged her back, but gingerly. Pellea pulled back to smile into her face.

"I know you have some resentments and I think we should air them fully right away. We can figure out what caused the misunderstandings and come to grips with them."

She hugged her friend again, then stepped back and looked serious.

"But first I need to tell you a few things. We spent a lot of time away from you, I know. We were on the continent, preparing for the invasion, and that took up all our time. And then there was the wedding." She looked into Kim's eyes, shaking her head with regret. "I wanted you in my wedding."

Kim blinked, wishing she didn't still have these feelings of doubt. "But you didn't send for me."

"Kim, I sent a request. In fact, we sent many requests. And every time, the Granvilli government refused. They said you couldn't be spared. And by then, most of the people I could trust seemed to have disappeared. I couldn't find anybody to use to get a message to you. We had to go ahead with the wedding without you. I had to have one of Monte's newfound cousins stand in for you. Look." She pulled out a beautiful wedding announcement card, printed on fine linen paper and decorated with elaborate calligraphy and showed it to her. There on the face of it she saw "Mandy Kraktus, standing in as Maid of Honor for Kim Guilder."

Kimmee stared at the card. She couldn't deny what it meant. Her eyes were shining when she looked up at Pellea again.

"Leonardo went insane when he heard you had married Monte," she told her.

Pellea shuddered. "So I've heard."

"And then you invaded and everything went crazy."

"Yes. People start to feel like it's every man for himself and then you don't know what they'll do." She hesitated, then looked at her friend sideways. "They say that you went into hiding with Leonardo."

Kim's short laugh was bitter. "That's one way to put it, I suppose."

Pellea's eyes flashed and she reached out to take Kim's hands in hers. "He took you to the chateau, didn't he?"

Kim nodded. "Yes."

"And kept you there for…"

Her hands tightened on Pellea's. "Pellea, believe me,

I didn't go willingly. But I'm not going to talk about what happened there."

"Oh, Kimmee…"

"What he did to me was mostly out of anger, rage, frustration at how he was losing his country. All things being equal, I would have loved to see him punished. But that can never be. Leonardo is my baby's father. And that is that. If I have my way, she'll never know even a fraction of what happened. It could only hurt her and scar her life. And I won't allow that." She took a deep breath, her gaze steely. "In fact, this is the last time I will ever speak of it. From now on, it's a lost chapter in my life."

Pellea had tears in her eyes and she hugged her friend tightly. "Oh, Kimmee. I'm so, so sorry. But I completely understand you on this and I promise to comply."

"Thank you." Kim looked over her shoulder at where Jake held Dede. He was looking at her with a strange light in his eyes and she blinked, trying to get a fix on it. Suddenly she realized what it was. Sympathy. Compassion. Understanding. And most of all, love.

Her heart jumped. Was she imagining it? No, there was something in his gaze that seemed to put a protective shield around her. He wanted to keep her safe. She could almost see his determination. She smiled, but he didn't smile back. Still, the connection between them was strong and real. A certain joy filled her and tears began to threaten again.

She turned back to Pellea as her friend reached out to touch her cheek lovingly. "How did you get away?" she asked.

"He got tired of me at last and let me go. He'd found someone else and lost interest in making my life a misery. And I left quickly and never looked back."

Pellea nodded, her eyes full of tragedy, but a smile fixed on her face. "Of course."

Kim closed her eyes as though putting all that behind her, then opened them again and looked more accusingly.

"And I want you to know that I sent you letter after letter telling you what was going on. Why didn't you answer? I would have given anything just for one answer, just to know someone understood."

"Kimmee, I didn't get any of those letters. I had no idea what you were going through until we got back here, and even then it took some time. We'd been back for weeks before one of the maids came to tell me she'd found a stack of letters in a cabinet in the library—letters to me that she thought I should take a look at. Come with me. I'll show you."

Kim followed her a few doors down the hall to the residential library. Pellea threw open the cabinet to reveal the letters. Only one had even been opened.

"I wanted to leave them this way so you would see that I never got them."

"Oh." Kim sank into a chair, tears rimming her eyes. "Pellea. And all that time I thought…" She shook her head. "I feel I've wronged you terribly."

"No, darling. We're the ones. We were on the edge of invasion and things were so confused and chaotic. What little communication we managed didn't get through to where you were. We should have known, we should have tried harder."

"Hush." Kim rose and hugged her best friend. "It's over." Then her face changed. "But beyond that, all this talk of DNA and my being a princess—tell me it doesn't mean a thing."

Pellea's beautiful eyes were wide with innocence. "But it's all true. That's what's so amazing."

Kim stared at her. Somehow it didn't seem so ridiculous when Pellea took it seriously.

"But never mind that now. We can talk about it later. What's important right now is that you understand how much we all love you." She kissed her cheek and smiled into her eyes. "And even more important, where's that little girl of yours? I want to meet her."

Jake was holding her and he stepped forward.

"What a duckling you are!" Pellea cooed, pinching her cheeks gently.

Pellea had heard all about Dede's problems. Jake had filled her in.

"We've got four pediatricians coming to see her tomorrow," she told Kim. "We'll see what they come up with. Surely at least one of them will know something."

Kim choked up. She couldn't even get out the words to say how grateful she was. Meanwhile Pellea showered Dede with love and admiration, and Jake gave Kim a look that said, "See?"

Kim did see. A bubble of happiness was growing in her chest, but she wasn't sure if she dared let it keep on going and fill every corner. She had to keep it contained, a little bit to the side, a little bit safe. She still wasn't sure she believed all this niceness and love. She had to keep herself just a little bit protected.

A little later, when she told Jake how she felt, he chided her.

"Kimmee, would you stop looking a gift horse in the mouth? Of course they love you even more now that they have found out you're their sister for real. It's only human. You can't fault them for that."

"Yes, but…"

"Why do you keep looking for the worm in the apple? I say, bite the apple and don't look."

She smiled. "Okay, Jake. You seem to have all the answers." She stretched her arms out above her head, feeling suddenly safe and luxurious, all at once. They were in the courtyard garden that was a part of her new chambers, and for the first time in months, she had a feeling things might work out after all. "We'll do it your way."

Dede was asleep. They were sitting on the huge sectional couch that filled one corner of her room. It was late. Jake would be leaving soon for his own rooms. And Kim realized, suddenly, that she didn't want him to go.

"Thanks," she said to him, almost shyly.

He raised an eyebrow. "For what?"

"For making me come back here."

He reached out and brushed hair back off her cheek, then let his fingers cup her ear. She looked at him, at his crystal-blue eyes, at his dark, slightly wavy hair, at the scrape on his face that was almost healed, at the full, sexy shape of his lips, and she knew what it was like to melt a little.

He moved toward her and she lifted her face. He kissed her lips softly, once, twice, and then one more time. She closed her eyes and yearned toward him, but he pulled back and the next thing she knew, he was lying on the couch with his head in her lap.

"How did this happen?" she asked him with a smile, threading her fingers through his thick hair.

"I don't know," he said. "Sometimes you've just got to do what comes naturally."

"Oh no, you don't," she said, teasing him. "I prefer a little civilization."

"Phony," he murmured at her.

She sighed and leaned back, enjoying the feel of him so close, enjoying the night. Was she in love? Was life calming down to the point where she could let herself be? She did love a lot of things about him. She loved that he was such a tough guy, and yet he was never harsh with her. She knew he wanted her. She wanted him. And yet she also knew he would take it easy, wait until she was ready. It all seemed so right.

And yet...

There was one ugly obstacle to everything and it was huge. Leonardo. She knew how he felt about the man. She felt the same way. But she also knew he couldn't get past it. There were feelings in him that he couldn't seem to get beyond. And that might mean they would never be able to get together the way they both might want to.

They talked softly for another half hour, and then it was time for him to leave. They lingered at the big wooden gate. His good-night kiss went on and on, until they were both out of breath and clinging together as though they couldn't bear to be apart. And when he finally left, Kim missed him before he even disappeared from sight.

Christmas was a lovely day with celebrations in the chapel and a feast in the main hall. There was a dance and plays performed and an old-fashioned jousting tournament. But through it all, Kim was anticipating the afternoon when the pediatricians were due to arrive. And though she enjoyed the festivities and soaked up Jake's growing signs of affection like a kitten in the sun, her focus was Dede.

At one point, Pellea took her into the library again to show her the documentation on the DNA evidence.

"There's no getting around it, Kim. It's all here in black and white."

"I don't get it. I never had a moment's doubt that Lady Constance was my mother."

"Then she did her job well." Pellea took her hand. "It was all done for your benefit, you know. They were all so afraid the Granvillis would kill you if they knew."

"Okay, tell me how you know that. How do you know what they were thinking at the time?"

She shrugged. "We have Queen Elineas' diary. She wrote it all down in her own hand."

"You mean…?"

"This was found a few months ago when tearing down a wall near what was the burned-out area from the original invasion. A worker found the diary in a small hiding place. You'll have to read it."

What a treasure! "I plan to."

"The queen tells of how she kept her pregnancy a secret, then enlisted Lady Constance to help her hide you. She was so afraid all her other children would be killed. She wanted one to carry on the name. And she thought that one might be you."

"Poor lady," Kim murmured. She wished she could feel closer, emotionally, to the old queen who might possibly be her real mother. But a lifetime of propaganda was hard to dispel so quickly.

"Indeed. Read the diary. I think you'll start to appreciate being a part of this family." She gave her an impish grin. "I know I have."

And she left, on to other duties, just being a queen. And Kim stayed and did some reading.

But finally she was in the examination room with

Dede while four physicians in white coats nodded gravely over her child and began to confer. Jake had come with her. She held his hand tightly and thought about how much his support was beginning to mean to her.

There were tests, tests and more tests for Dede. They needed to check internal organs and for that she had to be sedated. Kim didn't like it, but she gave permission. Then she had to leave her baby, which was very hard, and Jake took her away to have lunch in her courtyard. Pellea stopped by for a quick visit, and so did a couple of other friends from the old days. But her heart was with her child. It was late in the afternoon when they let her see her baby again.

And then, the verdict.

"Your baby has a low-grade infection and has had it for some time. It was perceptive of you to realize it was different from the normal baby complaints. It would have been better to start treatment long since, but all we can deal with is what we have before us. Ordinarily, we would check her into the hospital for a ten-day period of controlled antibiotics. But since you have such appropriate facilities in your living compound, we should be able to attend to her right here in the castle. With constant professional oversight, of course."

Kim's head was spinning.

"Don't worry," the pediatrician told her kindly. "This is eminently treatable. Left alone, it could prove debilitating in time. But you've brought her in and we're going to get to work on it. She'll be fine in no time at all."

Relief flooded her body and she hugged Jake as the doctor left the room.

She had to leave Dede in recovery for now. She and

Jake took a walk around the viewing level and talked softly, first about Dede, then about Kim's reaction to Pellea, and finally, about Jake's plans.

"I'm so glad you've been here to help me through all this," she told him. "I can't thank you enough."

He was silent for a moment, then he said, "Then I'd better warn you. I'm going away for a few days."

She turned in horror. "What? Why?"

"I have something I have to do and I…"

Her blood ran cold. "You're going to find Leonardo, aren't you?"

He took a deep breath. "Yes."

This was what she'd been dreading, even though she hadn't let herself focus fully on it. This was how the past could reach out and ruin things in the future. It wasn't fair. It made her want to scream.

"Jake, I hope you understand," she said carefully. "If you kill Dede's father, we can never be together."

The truth of that statement seemed to resonate in the cold air. And the central situation was starkly clear. Kim wanted Jake. She'd never known a man who seemed so right, so real for her.

And he wanted her. He'd only known her for a few days and she already filled his head and his senses. Things were possible here. They already had the beginnings of a real romance. With a little luck, they had the foundations of a real relationship.

But if he did this…

He knew that. Hatred of Leonardo consumed him, and not in a good way. He didn't like feeling this way. He wanted it over. There had been a time when he'd thought he couldn't love Kim because of it. And Dede, too. But now he knew that nothing about Leonardo had anything to do with either one of them. Leonardo had happened to them, the way he had happened to Jake and his family. All the rest was dust in the wind.

But he did have to take care of things. He couldn't leave it hanging. He had to go.

"Please, Jake," she whispered, tears welling in her eyes. "Please don't go."

"I have to go, Kim. It's a strange thing. Almost like destiny. I have to do this. Otherwise I'll never be able to live with myself."

"Jake…"

"Kim, he had my family killed. He has to pay for that. And what he did to you…how can you want me to let that go? He has to face up to what he did. And I have to make sure he never does that to anyone else."

She turned away. Either Leonardo would kill him, or he would kill Leonardo. She couldn't win. Either way, she was doomed. She drew in a shaky breath.

"When will you go?"

"Tonight. When it feels right. I want to cross the border before the first light."

She nodded, feeling strangely lightheaded. "Goodbye. Please be safe."

"Don't worry about me, Kim. I'll be back."

She hoped so with all her heart and soul. But if he came back as Leonardo's killer, everything would be over.

He saw the devastation in her eyes and he pulled her up and kissed her, hard, as though his heat and passion should convince her. And she kissed him back, just as hard, as though her love could persuade him. But they both failed. Sadly, she went back to her rooms alone.

It was almost dawn. Dede was fast asleep, exhausted by all the probing and testing and medication. Kim had slept earlier but now she was awake, and she knew she wasn't going to go back to sleep. Her mind was racing, trying to find a way out of what she was sure would be disaster. She knew Jake was already on his way back into Granvilli territory. There was nothing she could do. So why was the entire issue still roiling through her mind?

She was trying to keep busy, but it wasn't working. Two nurses had been assigned to watch over Dede for the night. They were both very nice and it was wonderful to have people who knew what they were doing care for her baby. But Kim couldn't help but feel a bit superfluous. If anything happened, she would be the one standing back and trying not to scream.

She wandered through the courtyard, from the rose garden to the mini forest, stopping to sit near the waterfall, then trying to see if she could find the secret passage Pellea and Monte had escaped through.

She heard one of the nurses get a call on her phone, but she hardly paid any attention until she heard the words, "Is he still alive?"

She looked up. The second nurse had come out into the courtyard and was watching the first take the call. They exchanged significant glances and the first nurse asked more questions.

Frowning, Kim made her way to where the two nurses were standing. "What's going on?" she asked.

"Oh, miss!" The first nurse turned to her excitedly. "They say…the word is…Leonardo Granvilli is dead."

Kim clutched her arm, filled with dread. "How? Where?"

"Near the border. They say it must have happened right around midnight. My friend says she heard he was seen in Dorcher Cliffs on Christmas day. They think he was trying to come in from that direction, but his body was found near the last roadblock. Multiple gun-shot wounds. Some say it's him, some say not." She shrugged. "We can only hope."

For just a moment, Kim couldn't breathe. Had there been enough time for Jake to get to the border? Yes. Plenty of time.

"Oh," she said, then clamped her hand over her mouth. "Oh! Oh!"

The nurse laughed. "Yes, it's wonderful. Isn't it? I mean, it's never nice to wish someone ill, but that man was pure evil and he ruined a lot of lives. Now we can go back to being one Ambria again. I'll get to go visit my sister in Tantarette."

Kim could hardly stand upright. She was weaving and she knew it. Time to get control.

"Will you be here for my baby?" she asked, stumbling over her words. "I mean, I have to go. Please, please, I don't want my baby left alone."

"Oh course, miss. We'll both be here. That's our job."

"Oh." Kim ran and shrugged into a huge furry jacket she found in the closet. "I'll be back as soon as I can. But not real soon."

"Take your time, miss."

Time. The term rattled in her brain. Where did she think she was going? What did she think she was going to do?

She didn't know. She only knew she had to try to find Jake. There would be soldiers looking for Leonardo's killer. She had to warn him. Someone had already done what he was going out to do.

At least, she hoped that was it. What if…what if the killer *was* Jake? What if he'd made a lucky move and found Leonardo just at the right time and…

No, she couldn't think about that. If he'd killed

Dede's father, life would be impossible in so many ways. But if he was just out there, not knowing the new danger he was facing….the soldiers looking for anyone who might have had anything to do with the killing…anyone who might have had a motive…. She had to try, at least. She had to find a way to warn him. For the moment, his safety was everything to her.

She made a futile attempt to use her new mobile to find him, but she knew in advance there was no coverage where he was going. If she was going to do this, it had to be the old-fashioned way.

She raced down the long stairway to the basement motor-pool bay. She'd spent most of her life in this castle and she knew how things worked. The lot would be filled with cars to choose from. There would be no one attending at this time of the morning. And she knew where the keys were kept. She would have her choice of fast cars.

She reached the basement and turned slowly, looking at all the shiny vehicles. What had Jake chosen for his dangerous journey back across the border? Something that could outrun the authorities or something inconspicuous that would let him slip past the guards unnoticed? Something he could easily ditch at the crossing so that he could go over on foot? Who knew? And how was she going to know it was him if she met his car on the road?

She swayed, suddenly overcome with hopelessness. This was a fool's errand, wasn't it? Finding him would be nearly impossible. What was she going to do? Tears of fear and frustration filled her eyes and she leaned against an ancient Bentley and sobbed. What in the world was she going to do?

A strangely familiar sound interrupted her tears, and

she lifted her head and listened. There was a sputtering, a feeble roar, and suddenly Jake came cruising into the parking garage, riding the decrepit motorcycle that had brought them out of Granvilli territory just days before.

Jake! Relief surged in her veins. He was alive, at least. But with all these wonderful cars to choose from, why would he have gone off on that old thing? And what had he done?

She ran to him and he quickly parked the bike, surprised to see her.

"Oh, Jake!"

He took her into his arms and held her close. "What is it?" he asked. "What's happened?"

She turned her tear-stained face up to him. "Oh Jake, I was so afraid that you…"

"Hush." He put his finger to her lips to stop her. "Before you say anything more, I have something to tell you."

"To tell me?" She blinked, dread back again. Had he done it? Was he the one?

"Yes. I want you to listen before you say anything at all. I want you to understand what I've done and why I've done it."

"Oh, no," she wailed, sure she knew exactly what he meant.

"Just listen." He dropped a soft kiss on her lips. "I left tonight, determined to find Leonardo and kill him. I felt I had to do it. I wanted to do it. Justice demanded I do it. The honor of my family demanded I do it. And I was ready."

"Oh Jake," she moaned softly, shaking her head in sorrow.

"I'd heard the intelligence that pinpointed his location. I knew where he was and where he was headed.

Everything was working out just right. So I felt pretty good as I rode along. I even chose our motorcycle as a sort of spiritual nod toward destiny. You understand?"

She nodded mournfully.

"But how did you get it?"

"Some of the local boys who scout around the border looking for useable items found it and brought it in. When I saw it, I couldn't resist."

"Oh, Jake."

"But the motorcycle isn't very fast, and as I made my way, I had a lot of time to think." He smiled down at her and raked his fingers through her hair, holding her head like a precious orb. "I'm not a killer, Kim. If I kill Leonardo, a part of me will be satisfied. But another part will open like an infected wound, a wound that won't have a way to heal. I'll lose you, I'll lose Dede, and what will I gain?"

He kissed her lips again, softly, sweetly, and she returned the kiss with a hunger that grew out of love.

"I finally had to come face-to-face with the truth," he went on. "I'd rather respect myself for decency than for vengeance. I'll work with any entity that aims to bring that foul man to justice, but I won't kill him with my own hands." He smiled down into her eyes. "I have to be a man you could love. Not a monster."

"Oh Jake," she sighed, melting against him. "I'm so glad. I'm so, so glad."

He kissed her as though it was his last chance, and she arched into his body with her own, wanting to feel him everywhere. A sound at the entry stopped them cold. Morning was coming. People would begin arriving.

"Let's go to my room," he murmured near her ear.

She nodded. "I've got something to tell you," she said, happiness sparkling in her eyes. "Come on."

They dodged early morning maids and footmen through the corridors, giggling and chuckling as they snuck past sleepy workers. They ended up at last in his dark outer room and he led her straight for the bedroom. She couldn't see a thing.

"Jake? Are you there?"

As her eyes grew more accustomed to the dark, he pulled her down onto the huge bed with white sheets and pillows and an enormous canopy.

His arms came around her and he was kissing her again, holding her tightly, breathing in her scent.

"Wait," she muttered, half laughing, half tempted to spend the rest of her life in his arms. "I have to tell you this. Guess what?" She could hardly talk as she was raining kisses all over him. He'd shrugged out of his jacket and his shirt was open and his wonderful chest was uncovered and vulnerable to all the attention she wanted to give it.

"Save the guessing games for later," he murmured, using his tongue to explore her ear.

"No, I'm serious. Listen. Everything's changed."

He took hold of her shoulders, holding her back a bit and protecting his ribs. "What's changed?" he asked groggily.

"Everything. You don't have to worry about bringing Leonardo to justice."

"What are you talking about?"

"Jake, they found his body. Either someone's already killed him or he's killed himself. So you don't have to."

He went very still. "Are you serious?"

"Yes. The news came in about an hour ago."

Jake shook his head as though trying to shake some reality into it. "He's gone?"

"Yes, that's what they are saying. I only hope it's true."

"Where? How?"

Quickly she ran over all the facts she knew. He heaved a huge sigh and she realized a part of him was disappointed.

She groaned. Men really were different, weren't they? She didn't care about revenge. She didn't care about anything much other than her adorable baby— and Jake.

Morning light was beginning to come through the window, enough so that he could see her beautiful face. He framed it with his hands, loving her. This was where his destiny lay. This was where he would build his life from now on. His heart filled with pure, sweet happiness and he smiled down at her.

"Dede?" he asked, suddenly remembering that she was still in jeopardy.

She nodded. "She seems to be fine. Or healing, at least. They all say so."

He nodded back, satisfied, and then he pulled her close again. "In the meantime, what are you doing in this huge furry jacket thing? I can hardly find the real you down under all this stuff."

She grinned. "You don't like it?"

"No. Not a bit."

"Then it goes." She pulled it off and tossed it aside.

He laughed. "Good. Now about that shirt…"

"It stays." She sighed, leaning close to kiss him again.

"Okay," he muttered. "As long as you stay, too."

He soaked in the look of her in the morning haze and managed to get her under the covers and curled up against him. She closed her eyes. She knew she couldn't get any closer to heaven without making the transition to angel—and that was a long way off.

"Jake?" she whispered.

"What?" he answered sleepily.

"I think I love you."

"Good. Let me know when you're positive."

"Jake?"

"What?"

"You're supposed to at least give me a hint."

"Oh. You mean, you want to know if I love you?"

"Exactly."

He tugged her closer and kissed her neck. "You'll do."

"Jake!"

He chuckled, deep in his throat. "I surrender, Kim. I love you, too. And I'm more sure than you are. So I win."

"Oh no, my darling Jake," she said, laughing as she cuddled in closer. "I win. I win it all."

* * * * *

Mills & Boon® Hardback

January 2012

ROMANCE

The Man Who Risked It All	Michelle Reid
The Sheikh's Undoing	Sharon Kendrick
The End of her Innocence	Sara Craven
The Talk of Hollywood	Carole Mortimer
Secrets of Castillo del Arco	Trish Morey
Hajar's Hidden Legacy	Maisey Yates
Untouched by His Diamonds	Lucy Ellis
The Secret Sinclair	Cathy Williams
First Time Lucky?	Natalie Anderson
Say It With Diamonds	Lucy King
Master of the Outback	Margaret Way
The Reluctant Princess	Raye Morgan
Daring to Date the Boss	Barbara Wallace
Their Miracle Twins	Nikki Logan
Runaway Bride	Barbara Hannay
We'll Always Have Paris	Jessica Hart
Heart Surgeon, Hero...Husband?	Susan Carlisle
Doctor's Guide to Dating in the Jungle	Tina Beckett

HISTORICAL

The Mysterious Lord Marlowe	Anne Herries
Marrying the Royal Marine	Carla Kelly
A Most Unladylike Adventure	Elizabeth Beacon
Seduced by Her Highland Warrior	Michelle Willingham

MEDICAL

The Boss She Can't Resist	Lucy Clark
Dr Langley: Protector or Playboy?	Joanna Neil
Daredevil and Dr Kate	Leah Martyn
Spring Proposal in Swallowbrook	Abigail Gordon

Mills & Boon® Large Print

January 2012

ROMANCE

HISTORICAL

MEDICAL

Mills & Boon® Hardback

February 2012

ROMANCE

HISTORICAL

MEDICAL

Mills & Boon® Large Print

February 2012

ROMANCE

The Most Coveted Prize	Penny Jordan
The Costarella Conquest	Emma Darcy
The Night that Changed Everything	Anne McAllister
Craving the Forbidden	India Grey
Her Italian Soldier	Rebecca Winters
The Lonesome Rancher	Patricia Thayer
Nikki and the Lone Wolf	Marion Lennox
Mardie and the City Surgeon	Marion Lennox

HISTORICAL

Married to a Stranger	Louise Allen
A Dark and Brooding Gentleman	Margaret McPhee
Seducing Miss Lockwood	Helen Dickson
The Highlander's Return	Marguerite Kaye

MEDICAL

The Doctor's Reason to Stay	Dianne Drake
Career Girl in the Country	Fiona Lowe
Wedding on the Baby Ward	Lucy Clark
Special Care Baby Miracle	Lucy Clark
The Tortured Rebel	Alison Roberts
Dating Dr Delicious	Laura Iding